FALLOUT

CAROLINE SPRINGS CHARTER
LILA ROSE

Second Edition 2019
ISBN: 978-0648481614

PROLOGUE

FANG

I'd just arrived back to the compound when Gamer told me I was needed in the back room. I knew what that meant. Something was going down.

Entering, I saw Alvin cowering near the wall with a combination of fear and disgust on his face. Christ, what had the idiot done now? "What's goin' on?" I asked.

"This boy here said some shit to Knife," Vicious explained.

"He was kissin' another dude, in front of everyone. Faggots, the lot—"

"Shut the fuck up," I snarled. My top lip pulled up from my teeth in revulsion. Stupid bigot motherfucker.

"You still vouchin' for him?" Dodge asked.

"Nope," I replied. Never really wanted to vouch for him as a prospect in the first place. Only did it for his old man. Charlie had been like a second father to me. He'd hoped Alvin would shape up and come to respect a club he wasn't a part of since, for some stupid reason— probably drugs fuckin' with his mind—Alvin hated his dad, and my old club, the Venom MC. Charlie also hoped the act of getting him in a club would straighten Alvin out. Looked like Alvin wasn't willing to change, and since he couldn't keep his mouth shut, he was about to be taught a lesson. A much-needed one. Been meaning to speak to Dodge about him, but we'd all been swamped with shit, and Alvin hadn't been around long as a prospect. Soon that'd end also, and I wouldn't have to see the dick again.

Knife looked at me with a smirk, and asked, "You think he'll piss himself?"

I snorted. "Could. Not that I care. I only brought him in as a favour to his father."

Alvin hissed through clenched teeth, "You let them touch me, you won't see my sister again."

Fury raced through me and I was on him in seconds. I gripped his tee and pulled him up to my face. "You touch Poppy, I'll fuckin' kill you."

The idiot snorted. "I don't have to touch her. Haven't

you noticed she ain't been around? It's 'cause dearest daddy has already had a taste, and he's willin' to share when I'm older."

My ears rang as my temper raised quickly. The room went silent.

He couldn't be serious. Charlie wouldn't touch Poppy. Logically I knew it, but his words rolled over in my mind again and again, and each time I heard them, I saw nothing but rage. Alvin paled before me as I roared my wrath in his face for making up such lies. I threw him into the wall. My fist smashed into his cheek first, then nose, gut, and face again. Alvin fell to the floor.

Breathing heavily, I glanced over my shoulder, my eyes dead. "He's all yours," I stated, before making my way to the door. I needed to get to the bottom of why Alvin would say that. I needed to see Poppy, make sure she was okay. The *need* consumed me.

"Fang, don't go in it alone."

I paused at Dodge's words. My hand tightened on the door handle. "Don't know what you're talkin' about," I replied, before I threw the door open and stalked out.

My fist clenched when I heard, "Fuck. Vicious, Muff, Pick, after him. Take his back."

CHAPTER ONE

FANG

My head thumped, and each time it pulsated at my temples, I wanted to punch something. No, I wanted to beat the ever-loving shit out of someone. Alvin Torian was one lucky mother-fucker that I was walking away from him. But I had to because Alvin's lie had to be just the drugs talking, and if I'd kept going, I wasn't sure if Poppy or Charlie would forgive me. I knew Alvin was high most of the time, another reason Charlie got Alvin away from the Venom club. Some members still dabbled in selling on the side apparently, and they still would until Blackie, the president of the club, got his shit together and either enforced the rule or kicked them out. Blackie wanted a clean club to some extent, though he still dealt with whores, but other than that, he wanted a fresh start.

The shit Alvin was spewing was just that. Shit. Charlie was second in command and he'd been the one to push for a clean path for the Venoms. Charlie wouldn't hurt a fly unless someone was hurting or touching one of his. Then it'd be on, and Charlie wasn't one to back down.

Fuck Alvin for the crap he pulled.

It wasn't true.

It'd never be true. Not with Charlie and his daughter, Poppy.

Christ. Poppy.

I'd known her for ten years, since we were teens and in high school.

Goddamn was she adorable back in the day. Glasses, frizzy red hair, and rock chick clothes. She used to get so flustered every time I was near and always made me grin. Hell, I'd even go out of my way to see what she'd say or do next.

Yeah, she'd been damn cute, and I'd claimed her as my friend because I'd wanted to be close to her. There was just something about Poppy Torian that dragged me in.

And since we'd grown, she'd turned into a stunner. I'd only seen her the once. It was a while ago, since she'd come back from university, and it hadn't been a good time. I'd been out at a nightclub with Vicious and Nary....

Christ, Nary was another story. A love I'd lost to my brethren because I'd been stupid to think she'd eventually love me. She had, but it was never a strong hold like she'd had for Vicious. Which was why I'd stepped back, that and the guilt I still held over Nary being taken in the first place. Thank fuck they were both in a good place. Finally.

Motherfucking hell. I ran a hand over my face. My mind was messed up. My thoughts jumped from one to another. I needed my head clear, and thinking about losing Nary *and* Poppy wasn't going to help me any.

That was the truth of it.

I'd lost Poppy too. She'd left without telling me and refused to take my calls. I didn't understand why. *I still don't.* Which could be why I didn't chase her after that first sighting in the nightclub.

Back then, she was too young, yet I still wanted her. I'd longed for her to be on the back of my bike, in my bed, and heart. I still did.

But when I'd seen her, her eyes had shone with hurt. It confused the fuck out of me.

It didn't make sense.

"Poppy." I smiled down at her as I stopped beside her at the bar. Her body stiffened at the sound of my voice.

She shifted her head slightly to the side. "Hey," she replied, and then went back sipping her drink.

Smirking, I mentioned, "No glasses."

"Contacts."

I didn't like her short reply. "What, you're not gonna talk to me?"

Sighing, her chin dropped to her chest and then she straightened to face me. "What do you want?"

She was cold and distant. I didn't understand it. We'd been friends before she'd gone. Before she'd left me. Didn't stop my eyes travelling over her frame noticing her tits, arse, and the extra weight she carried around her hip-hugging jeans. The top few buttons on her tight shirt were undone so I could see her cleavage clearly. Shit, I wanted to see what was under her clothes. My hands itched to reach out and take hold of her waist, dragging her to me to taste her sweet plump lips.

Forcing a laugh, I said, "What do you mean what do I want? Haven't seen you in a while, babe. How you been?" I started off simple, trying to get to the bottom of why she goddamn left in the first place. And more specifically, why she'd left me.

She rolled her eyes. "Good, Fang." She spat out my club name like it was a dirty word. "But I got places to be, drinks to have, and men to grope."

Narrowing my eyes, I bit out, "What the fuck, Poppy? What's with the attitude? How you think Blackie or Charlie would like the cold way you're acting?"

"Whatever, I don't have time for this." She spun and stalked away.

My body unlocked and I was after her. Catching up, I gripped her arm. She spun and hissed, "Fuck off, Fang." As I was about to get in her face, she opened her mouth again. "You left the club. You have no right to say what I can and can't do. Now leave me the fuck alone." She yanked her arm free and made a run for the entrance. I'd been too frozen to do anything, not sure I understood where the toxic tone and attitude came from. If I were to guess, it had to do with me leaving the Venom MC, the one her family was a part of. Did she see that as me leaving her? Our friendship? Christ, that couldn't be it, not considering what she put me through by blocking me from her life.

I should've gone after her and had it out, but I hadn't, and I'd left it too long. Why I'd left it so long, I didn't know, but it wasn't like that scene and Poppy weren't on my mind all the time. They were.

Anyway, she would have known I left the Venom MC because of my father.

She probably hated me already. But I'd soon change that and get to the bottom of her problem. Just like I'd find out what her fuckface of a brother was going on about.

Should have made my move a long time ago, but I didn't, and I could no longer stay away. Something in me had me gunning for my bike with a desire to see she was okay.

"Fang," Vicious called.

Ignoring him, I kicked my ride to life and revved her hard a few times before I put my helmet on and took off.

I saw in my side mirror my brethren running for their own rides to follow. But I was already in the wind.

I PULLED up at the kerb to Poppy's parents' place. It was the only place I knew to look. If she wasn't around, then I'd have a few words with Charlie about his cunt of a son. After making my way to the door, I pounded my fist on it and glanced behind. The roar of my brothers' rides grew louder and then shut off when they were parked alongside mine. Vicious, Muff, and Pick headed my way. I faced the door and hit it again with the side of my fist. Just as the brothers reached me, I raised my fist to bang at the door again, but it opened before my hand could touch it.

In it stood a furious Poppy.

She might have been furious, but I could still tell she'd been crying. Her eyes were red and puffy, her nose pinked at the sides from blowing it. Something was wrong.

A strangled choke from behind had me glancing over my shoulder to see Muff's gaze was running over Poppy's body. Quickly I turned back and my own eyes widened.

She was in a towel.

Just a towel.

A short one at that.

Spinning back to my brothers, I clipped, "Fuck off."

Vicious smirked, and I wanted to wipe it off his face. "We'll wait by the bikes. Call us if you need us."

"I don't mind stayin'," Muff commented, trying to glance around to Poppy *in a goddamn towel.*

It was lucky Pick grabbed the back of Muff's tee and led him roughly away from the house or he would have gotten a taste of my fist down his fucking throat.

My gaze stayed on them until I saw they were at the rides. Poppy cleared her throat. At least I hoped she was clearing it and not growling at me. Though either way it was cute as hell.

Facing her, I let my gaze run over her quickly. My cock throbbed behind my jeans at the sight of her bare skin. I was enjoying what I saw, even though my brothers were there and she looked about ready to murder me with her scowl and arms crossed over her chest. A chest I wanted a better look at.

"What's wrong?" I asked, meeting her stare.

"Are you seriously here to ask me what's wrong? What are you doing, Fang?"

"Jerimiah," I growled.

She seemed stunned for a second before her wide eyes change back to a glare. "I have things to do, *Fang*. I thought whatever you had to say was urgent with the way you were banging on the door. Tell me and then go so I can finish getting dressed."

Clenching my teeth in annoyance, I breathed out my nose deeply. My Poppy had changed. She never used to give me such attitude. Not that I wasn't liking it. I just didn't understand the change. She used to be sweet, shy, and happy. What was going on? "Poppy, why have you been crying?"

"*Fang*, why are you here?"

"Poppy," I barked.

"Fang," she snapped.

"Fucking hell." I ran a hand through my hair in frustration. "Is your dad here?"

Shit. Her bottom lip trembled. Alvin couldn't have been right. I wouldn't fucking believe it until I heard it. I couldn't be rash, so the fury building inside of me had to hold until I got to the bottom of everything.

"No. He's drinking alone at the pub."

My head jerked back. Charlie never went drinking during the week. He kept it to the weekends, and only around his brothers at the Venom compound.

Reaching out, she backed up. With a sigh, I begged, "Baby, please, tell me what's going on."

She sniffed, her chin jutting out. "Just leave."

"Poppy—"

"I don't concern you anymore, Fang. You've made that clear." I winced. Fuck, she couldn't have heard me saying shit that night. Had she? *Jesus.* "Get out, get back on your ride and stay away."

"No."

Tears welled in her eyes. "I don't need this right now, Fang. Just leave, please," she whispered.

"We're friends—"

She snorted. "We used to be." She shook her head, her eyes closing for a moment. I just about had my hand on her arm when her eyes sprung open and hardened. She removed her hands from the towel and pushed at my chest, only to growl low in her throat when I didn't move.

"Get out," she yelled.

"No."

"Fuck off," she screamed, fisting my tee and trying to shove me again.

"No."

She sniffed, her head dropped forward. "Go."

"Poppy, please just tell me what's goin' on. I can help."

She shook her head, again and again. "You can't," she whispered.

"I might be able to."

Her shoulders shook. Christ, she was crying. My gut bottomed out.

"Poppy," I murmured. I lifted my hands to wrap around her wrist where she still gripped my tee, then traced circles with my thumb on her skin. "Baby, what's goin' on?"

She sucked in a loud breath and straightened. She

released my tee and stepped back again. "Why do you care?" she asked the floor, and before I could answer, she went on. "I'm a nuisance. I mean nothing to you, so I don't understand why you're here."

Fucking hell. She had been there and heard me that night. I'd been drunk and trying to get in the pants of some bimbo I couldn't even remember the name of. I'd had a huge fight with my dad and had needed space, needed to forget. Had to get Poppy out of my mind because she was younger than I was.

Christ. She wasn't supposed to hear that.

"I didn't mean it. You know—"

She scoffed and roughly wiped at her face. "None of it matters anymore."

"It does. It explains a lot. I didn't understand why you left to finish out school at your aunt's and never spoke to me again. Hell, if it was because of that, fuck, baby, I didn't mean it. I was drunk. Stupid."

"Don't call me that."

I threw up my hands, "What?"

"Baby. Never call me that."

"Poppy, is that why you never returned my texts or calls? Why you haven't seen me since you've been back?"

Pain slashed through her features, but there was something else as well... guilt. But for what? The pain I could understand, but the guilt, no way.

She shook her head, blanking her expression. "No,

Fang. I was a silly girl back then." My gut tightened. "A girl who thought the world of a guy and in her eyes, he could do no wrong. Then he gutted her. And then…." She closed her eyes, tears leaked out.

"And then what?" I asked, but my mind was stuck on one thing.

What exactly had I said that night? I knew some of it, but obviously not all. The pain written all over Poppy had my throat thickening.

"Nothing." She sniffed. "God, just leave… just go."

"Poppadom, what's goin' on?" came from behind me. Turning, I found Charlie standing there with furrowed brows until he saw it was me. Then he smiled. Hadn't seen him in for-fuckin'-ever and had only just spoken to him over the phone a couple of times about getting Alvin into Hawks. "Fang. Jesus, son. It's good to see you." When my hand came up to ward off my approaching brothers, he glanced there, then back, and asked, "What's goin' on?"

"We gotta talk, Charlie." I sensed Poppy take her leave, and I let her. She needed away from me, so I gave her space. *For now.* Until I found out what was going on, there was jack shit I could do. But I'd figure this out, work out how to fix it, and then in turn, fix Poppy and me.

CHAPTER TWO

POPPY

*S*eeing Jerimiah was too much. He'd been my rock, my everything really from the moment I'd moved to Caroline Springs and started at the same high school he went to.

It could have been my young, foolish feelings, but he'd been the love of my life… until he wounded me deeply.

When I left to heal, he'd called, texted a few times, but that didn't last long.

What he never did was come and see me.

He hadn't cared that much about me, and I'd had to come to terms with that. Him showing up on my doorstep, dragging up the past threatened to undo every piece of armour I'd erected to protect myself.

He could never know the other reason I left... to protect him.

Seeing Jerimiah left my mind spinning and remembering how it started.

PAST

My worst nightmare had come true. It was my first day at a new school, the first day of grade seven.

As I walked down the hall with my belly eating at my other intestines, it felt like everyone was staring at me. Almost as if I was something out of *Monster High*.

Note to self: Poppy, don't mention Monster High *to others. Then they'll really think you're an idiot like your brother does.* I wouldn't have cared what people thought that I still collected and liked *Monster High*, but I didn't have much going for me in the looks department, so I knew if they ever found out, I'd be an outcast for sure. Right then, I was glad my older brother, Alvin, refused to go to the same school as me. He'd be worse than anyone else in teasing me, just so people would like him more. I was also praying I'd last through the first day without any trouble.

Girls were bitches. *Shit, I shouldn't cuss. My mum hates it when I do.* She'd told me a million times over I was a lady and ladies didn't swear. So I tried real hard not to curse. However, they kept on slipping out. It was Mum's fault in a way. She was the one who married a man, my dad, who used foul words like it was his own personal language.

Speaking of bitches—*oops, another slip*—there were three girls standing down the end of the hall looking at me like I'd just peed in their lunch boxes. Great, so I was already on the radar of the ones who I'd usually steer clear of. I could only wish they were checking out the new school meat, meaning me, and leave me alone in the end. I liked to fly under the radar. I was used to it. At my old school, I had one friend, and we stuck to ourselves, which suited us. The bullies eventually left us alone, after growing bored with us.

Would the same go for here?

I wasn't sure.

But I kept my fingers crossed.

Glancing at the piece of paper in my hand again, I then looked at the lockers beside me and finished walking down to locker 505. The lady at the front desk, with a name I didn't remember, had said it wouldn't be hard to find, and she'd been right. The school was big, but thankfully, there were signs stating things along the way.

After adjusting my backpack over my shoulder, I dialled in my combination. I'd just gotten my locker opened when, for some reason, I slid my gaze to the right.

That was when I saw him.

He would have to have been at least a few years older than me, so maybe grade nine, and he stood out more than any other guy.

My body responded at the sight of him. My hands were first... they shook, so I gripped my locker door tightly and held on. Then my legs wobbled, my skin broke out in goosebumps, and I was certain if I could count my pulse, it was beating way faster than it should have been.

All that because he smiled at one of his friends.

I'd admired *some* guys before, which was normal, but my reaction to him was more.

It sounded silly, even to myself, but he was like one of those rock stars I had posters of on my walls at home. Tall, dark, and messy hair... smooth, tanned, and clear skin, and perfect white teeth. I wondered what colour his eyes were. He was too far down the hall so I couldn't see them properly. Though, I wanted to.

My body was shoved forward. My head hit the locker's edge. I cried out, but then bit my bottom lip. I couldn't let anyone see they affected me.

Turning, I came face-to-face with the three bitches. *Huh, figures.* I wanted to snort at how cliché they were about to be, because I seriously knew what was coming, a warning of some kind. I slipped my bag to the floor, in case I needed to use my arms in any way. I didn't make a sound and stared back, crossing my arms over my chest. When none of them said anything, I rose one brow, and that brought me a sneer from the middle girl.

She hissed low, "I don't like you looking at what's mine. Keep your eyes down, fugly."

God, so her play was to warn me away from the guy down the hall. Great, I must have been obvious with my ogling. I had to make sure I never got caught again.

The girl looked about my age, only more pronounced in the boob area. She dressed to show them off also, which told me she was a hussy. Easy. And a guy like the one I'd been gazing at probably took notice of her push-up bra and tarty ways. He was a teen after all, and my dad warned me about guys his age. That they'd only be after one thing and that was to get in your panties.

However, I couldn't blame her claiming him in that way. He was dream-worthy. Hell, if he was to ever be mine—*ha ha!*—I may even have had the courage to fight for him, instead of just protecting myself.

"Are you dumb as well as ugly?" a friend of hers asked. "Tell Nicky you get her."

Pushing my glasses up my nose, I nodded and curled my arms around my stomach.

They all looked me up and down. Then Nicky laughed. "Really, I shouldn't be worried about you. But

I'm sure Jerimiah would hate someone like you even looking at him. So I guess, I'm doing him a favour. If I see your eyes on him again, you'll be screwed." With that, she shoved my shoulder hard, and I was knocked back into the lockers again. When she stalked off down the hall heading towards Mr Rock Star, I was brave enough to give her the finger.

Jerimiah saw her coming and used that smile on her. *Gag.*

It was then I knew he would only be eye candy. No guy who liked girls like Nicky was worth even talking to. I rolled my eyes. It wasn't like he'd talk to me in the first place. Even on the off chance he did, I had a feeling I wouldn't want to hear what came out of his mouth anyway.

"Skanks, that's what they are." I glanced to my left to find a girl with honey-coloured hair leaning against a locker next to mine. She nodded to the scene down the hall. "Girls who're pretty, but shallow, are skanks to me." Her dark blue eyes met mine, and she smirked. "Not that I'd tell them that."

An unexpected laugh erupted from within me. "No. It'd be better if you didn't."

"Exactly. Hi, I'm Manda." Her hand came out. I took it and shook, an unusual move between girls our age, but I liked it at the same. She seemed nice enough, and she'd called Nicky and her friends skanks, which meant a lot because it meant she was smart, like me.

"I'm Poppy. It's nice to know all girls here aren't like them." I quickly picked up my bag and placed it in my locker after I got my first book out before turning back with my schedule.

"There are only a few who aren't. Don't worry, I'll help you along the way." She glanced down to the paper in my hand with my classes printed on it. "What class are you in?"

Pushing up my glasses again, I reread it and said, "Seven A. You?"

"Same." She grinned, and I returned it. "Sit with me?"

"I'd like that."

"But first we have to go to the all-school assembly."

Groan. I hated assemblies. Too many idiots in one room.

MANDA ENTERED THE GYMNASIUM FIRST. I took in what she was wearing to see if I would be out of place since the school didn't have a uniform policy. Manda was dressed in jeans and a red tee, which looked great with her hair. I was glad I'd picked jeans and tee too, though my T-Shirt was a black vintage KISS one.

Jutting my bottom lip forward, I blew my red frizzy

hair out of my face and slowly followed Manda. Well, it would have been slow if other students weren't pushing their way in around me and knocking me about.

Manda waited at the back row of seats. Each row dipped lower until it flattened out at the bottom for the basketball court. On the court was a movable podium and standing on it was the principal, whom I'd met when my dad and I looked around the school. With him were four other teachers, all sat in seats behind the main guy standing at a microphone.

"Come on, the seats are filling up," Manda said.

My heart raced in my chest. There were so many students. I was new, so they'd stare, and I hated the thought of it.

Manda had already descended some steps. With my head down, I quickly moved to follow. I didn't want to lose sight of her and have to sit by someone I didn't know. Not that I really knew Manda either, but she'd been nice so far.

My new friend stopped about halfway down, and in my scurry to keep up, I didn't see the foot come out. I tripped, arms out. I headed for the stairs knowing I was going to break something. My heart in my throat, knowing I wouldn't stop at just the fall but roll down the rest and injure myself even more.

That was until an arm came around my waist and I was spun back to my feet.

"Nicky, don't be a bitch" was growled over my head.

If my heart wasn't already beating fast, it would have been then. The voice was rough and deep.

"I didn't do anything, Jerimiah."

Jerimiah.

Shit.

Nicky'd said the name of the rock god I'd been staring at earlier and it'd been Jerimiah.

Crap, I was currently in the arms of Jerimiah.

If my nerves weren't eating at me, I would have looked up, maybe smiled and thanked him for his rescue, while commenting on his strong arms with a giggle. But I was a rattled nutcase being so close to him and nearly falling on my face in front of everyone in the first place. All because of his girlfriend.

Instead, I stepped back. His arm fell from around my waist, making me regret my move. Did he really need his firm, warm arm? I could have kept it there all day long if I just cut it off him.

God, what was I thinking?

Flicking my gaze up for a second, I gasped, then coughed on the air when I saw his dark eyes were already on me, and I quickly looked away. "Thanks," I mumbled, then turned and bolted for the spare seat next to Manda.

She was staring at me with her mouth wide as I plonked down and sank deeper into the seat. My cheeks would match a fire-engine red, or my hair, and the whispers around me weren't helping my blush settle at all.

However, even through the volume of everyone already gossiping, I still heard Nicky's snappy tone and Jerimiah's deep one barking back.

"That was epic," Manda whispered.

How was it epic? I didn't understand. All I knew was that I was the centre of attention and I didn't like it at all.

"Don't you think?" she pressed.

"Um, how was it epic? I nearly face-planted on the floor in front of everyone on my first day of school. Nothing epic about my embarrassment."

She giggled and leaned in more. "You don't get it. Jerimiah is like a movie star around here. Even the older popular guys want to be like him. Having him save you *and* calling Nicky out on it was *epic*. It'll be talked about for years to come."

Oh shit.

My belly twisted. The small breakfast I'd had threatened to make an appearance. That was all I needed, to vomit in front of everyone. I wanted to crawl under my chair and stay there until people stopped talking about it, about me.

I also wanted to glance over my shoulder, since I knew he was close, and take my fill. He was taller up close. The top of my head had only reached his collarbone. He was broader as well and built like a footballer.

Of course, the attraction I had for him amped up.... I could even say I fell for him a little then. Only I knew liking him as much as I did, without even really knowing him, was going to bring me nothing but trouble... or heartache.

CHAPTER THREE

PRESENT

FANG

Charlie ushered me further into the house and then followed me inside, closing the door behind him. "Will your guys be all right out there?"

"Yeah, they're good."

He nodded, and then made his way further into the living room. I followed. Once he'd sat in the worn armchair, I took a seat on their couch to his left. Charlie leaned back, ran a hand over his face and sighed.

"Fuck, Fang. Fuck." He shook his head, sadness in his eyes.

"Talk to me."

"Not that it ain't good to see you, son. But why are you here? My girl said you've been too busy to come around here anymore."

My nostrils flared as I clenched my jaw. "We'll get to that in a second. First, need to know what's goin' on around here, Charlie."

He nodded, clasping his hands over his gut. "It's my Mary." *Shit. Poppy's mum.* "She ain't doin' well, son. Got dementia. Had it for a while. We didn't know. It's gotten worse, and she's in care and… fuck, she forgets to eat and drink. She doesn't trust people, or forgets who they are sometimes. Even us."

Jesus Christ.

Mary had been the glue to the family, such a warm, loving person.

"Charlie, I… shit, I don't know what to say."

He looked to the hall towards the bedrooms. "Poppy ain't been handling it. Cuts her deep every time she visits her mum, especially when Mary doesn't remember her. Hell, none of us have been dealing well. Poppy came home a while back to help out a little."

Shifting, I leaned forward, my elbows on my knees. "Why didn't you tell me, Charlie?"

He winced. "Poppy asked me not to. Don't know what went on with you two, but—"

My hand shot up. "Mixed messages we need to sort out."

His brows rose. "So you gonna stick around? For her?"

Leaning back, I grunted. "She couldn't get rid of me even if she tried." *Not now. No way in fuck now.*

"Good to hear, son. Good to hear."

I'd been stupid to fight what I'd felt for her back in the day. So goddamn stupid. Yeah, we'd been young back then, but I could've made it work. Fuckin' wished I'd have admitted my feelings aloud. Risked it. If she'd felt the same way, things would've been different. She wouldn't have left. At least I didn't think she would have.

We'd been close as friends, but I only ever thought that was how she'd seen me. As her friend. A better brother to the one she'd had.

Back then, I'd also been scared to have Poppy around my dad. He'd been into young girls, and I used to see the way he looked at my girl. My Poppy. So if he saw I was interested in her in more ways than just friends, he would have made a play for her. Fucking sick mother-fucking cunt.

Then she'd left and wouldn't return my texts or calls. It'd gutted me. Then I'd got pissed at her cutting me out like she had. However, after some time, I thought it'd been for the best to have her outta my life and away from under his eyes. It'd hurt not hearing from her, though, but it was safer.

Safer until I got out from under him, which I finally was. He disappeared after shit went down with Hawks. But back then, I'd met Nary, and she'd been a welcome distraction. Nary was so much like Poppy in some ways, being shy and sweet. Didn't realise my feelings for Nary would grow so fast, but they had. Hell, I never thought I'd get over losing Nary. That was until I saw my Poppy again and my body, mind, and heart knew Poppy had never been forgotten.

All I had to do was fight for her, to show her I was meant to be in her life. I just fuckin' prayed I hadn't left it too long. She needed me more than ever with what she was going through, so I'd make sure I'd be there in any way I could.

"So, how's Alvin goin' with the Hawks?" Charlie asked, breaking through my thoughts.

Fuck.

I didn't feel like shitting all over his already upsetting situation, so I said, "Fine."

I forgot Charlie could read me. "What did the little prick do now?"

"Charlie—"

"No, Fang. You tell me."

Rubbing a hand on the back of my neck, I nodded.

"He's still doin' drugs and said somethin' foul to a brother. They're probably teachin' him a lesson right about now for it."

Charlie gave me a chin lift, his eyes dark. "Never should'a asked you to take him under your wing. He was messed up before Mary went into care and then became more so when we had to admit her. He's never been a good nut, but I still held out hope. Gotta hope for your own kids, right?"

"Yeah, Charlie."

"Christ. Mary'd hate Alvin for this. Fuckin' up a good chance like you gave him, and all because I'd asked. Sorry, Fang."

"All good. Nothin' on your back, Charlie."

"He's my flesh and blood, son."

"He may be, but he didn't learn, listen, or take on anythin' you tried with him. That ain't your fault. It's his and his alone. You think I'll be like my dad one day?"

"Fuck no," he snarled. Yeah, he'd known my father since he'd joined Venom when my dad was the prez of the club.

"Then Alvin's actions aren't anything against you. They're just his actions, his mistakes, and his lies."

Charlie's brows raised. "What you mean lies?"

Bad fucking move on my part.

"Nothin', Charlie."

"Fang."

"Just let this one fly, yeah?"

"Can't. Must have been a good lie for it to bring you here in the first place."

"Charlie—"

"Fang, seriously. Not sure where we went wrong with him, but I know what he's like, and it fuckin' kills me he's the way he is. But I need to know what he did."

"Fuck," I clipped, running a hand through my hair. Sighing, because I knew he wouldn't leave it alone, I said, "He called some Hawks faggots. Said the reason why Poppy wasn't around was because…. Christ, Charlie. He said you were doing shit with her and he'd be sharing her with you soon."

His body locked. His jaw ticked.

"My head wasn't right when he said it, and I saw red. I took a few shots at him before I left to come here. He's with the Hawks brothers at the compound, but knowin' them, he'll be in hospital soon. He was high, Charlie. Know that ain't an excuse but—"

His nostril flared. "You believed him?"

"For one second, before I laid a hand on him, then I knew he was talkin' outta his arse because I *know* you and Poppy. So I had to teach him a lesson for talkin' crap."

"He's dead to me."

I understood why, but Charlie had a big heart, and I didn't want him to make any rash decisions. "Charlie, he wasn't—"

His hand came up, his eyes clouding with anger. "Don't even fuckin' try, Fang. He knows what we're goin' through with his momma, yet he can lay a nasty lie like that out there for people to hear? He's goddamn dead to me. You pass that along. You get it to your brothers and make sure he knows if I see his face again, he'll regret it. You hear me, son?"

"Got you, Charlie."

"Good. Now what in the hell are you gonna do about my girl?"

"Win her over," I admitted.

"It'll take time."

"Got time."

"Good. Son, like to ask you to stick around, but I'm fuckin' furious still and the only way to calm me the hell down is to see my woman." He stood and mumbled to himself as pain flashed over his face. "Just hope to everythin' she knows who I am this time."

Fuck. I hated what Poppy and Charlie were goin' through.

He walked me towards the front door, calling out to Poppy he'd be back later. I didn't catch what she replied with, but Charlie must have because he kept going on out the front, locking the house behind him. He saw me watching and smirked, then sent a chin lift to my waiting brothers and got in his car, taking off.

"What's goin' on?" Pick asked when I arrived at their sides.

"He wants a message to get to Alvin."

"Done." Muff nodded. "What is it and I'll go there now."

"Alvin's dead to Charlie. Doesn't want to see his face again, and if he does, Alvin will regret it."

"So it was all bullshit?" Vicious asked. Wasn't sure why the fucker was there. I thought he still hated me, so it was a surprise he followed through with Dodge's order to have my back.

"Knew it was before I hit him, but I had a feelin' something else was goin' down." I glanced back to the house, grinding my teeth together. "Mary, the mum, she's been taken into care, got dementia."

Curses sounded all around from my brethren.

"What's the next move then?" Muff asked.

"You get to wherever Alvin is, replay the message, that's all I know for now."

"And you?" Vicious asked, and I was sure I saw a lip twitch before he went back to frowning.

"You guys can go," I stated with a glare.

Muff grumbled, "Shit. You guys have all the fuckin' luck. If you don't—" I sliced my eyes to him, his hands came up. "Got it, off limits."

After they'd disappeared, I made my way back towards the house, only that time I diverted off to the side and opened the gate there. Poppy's room was the same one it'd been all those years ago. Christ, walking to it brought back the memory of when I'd first snuck in.

PAST

I stood at the back of the room wishing I was anywhere but here. My fuckin' father had dragged me along. We were at the new member's house for dinner. We didn't really do dinners, but apparently, his woman had wanted to meet the prez of the club, aka, my dick of a father. With dinner over, the older men sat talking in the living room, while I stood at the back getting bored. There was Charlie, the new guy, Dad, and Blackie, the VP.

Then the front door burst open, and I was shocked to hell when the new girl from school barged in, clutching a backpack to the front of her. She gripped it like her life depended on it. It was when she froze, after turning around from closing the door, that I saw she'd been crying.

"Poppy?" Charlie said, standing.

She wiped her face, straightened, and then cleared her throat. "Sorry, um, I thought you were out tonight, Dad."

"What's going on?" he demanded.

"Nothing, ah…." She glanced at the other two men—she hadn't seen me leaning against the wall—and then back to her dad. I didn't miss the way my cunt of a father ran his eyes over her, and I wanted to gut him for it. I knew he liked younger women, but she was only fuckin' fourteen. She cleared her throat again. "It's nothing, just, ah, girl stuff." She nodded to herself.

Her dad blanched. I could tell it was a lie though from the trembling of her bottom lip and the way she looked everywhere but at them. Hell yes, she'd just fibbed. And for some goddamn reason, I wanted to know the real reason why she'd been crying.

"Yeah, uh, okay." Charlie nodded. "Before you disappear or talk to your mum, meet the president of the Venom Motorcycle Club, Switch. The vice president, Blackie, and Switch's son, Jerimiah."

I thinned my lips instead of laughing my arse off when I saw her reaction at hearing my name. Her eyes popped wide, her mouth dropped, and her body tensed. Then slowly, so slow in a way I wanted to bust a gut laughing, she turned to me, and then I heard her suck in a sharp breath.

I nodded to her. "Poppy." My lips twitched since I was still refraining from chuckling. Her face flushed. I had a feeling she'd be embarrassed about mentioning girl problems in front of me. Strange part was how she hadn't been concerned about it in front of the older men.

"Room. Bedroom," she blurted. Was that an invitation? Nope. Her eyes widened even more. "I'm, um…" She blinked slowly at me, then shifted back to face her father. "Nice to meet you all. I'm going to my bedroom now for the rest of the night." She bolted out of there like she was on fire.

It killed me not to follow her, but I knew if I showed an interest in Poppy, the girl with the wild red hair and bangin' body, my father would do something to mess with me. So I waited for a while and then told him I had to get outta there for a date. I *was* sixteen after all. He dismissed me with a grunt, while Blackie gave me a chin lift, and Charlie sent me a wave with a smile.

Out the front, I silently went through the side gate and down the house until I saw the light on at the end. It was either where Mary, Charlie's woman was, or Poppy's room.

Poppy. I hadn't known her name the day I'd helped her when Nicky tripped her up. I wanted to know it. Seeing her stunning-as-hell eyes when she'd eventually looked up did something to me, but she was young. Too young. Still didn't mean I had to be a dick. If someone was messing with her, I wanted to know and help her deal with it. After all, her family was a part of the club and we helped each other out.

I snuck a peak around the corner of the window and found Poppy pacing her room. She stopped abruptly, fisted her hands, stomped, and hissed something up at the roof.

Shit. It was cute.

Again, she started pacing away from the window. I stepped into view, and when she turned back, I heard her scream. Her hands went to her chest, and her mouth snapped closed while I smirked at her. Then her finger came up, which told me to wait. She went to her door opened it slightly and said something with a smile. Closing the door, she turned back to me and came to the window. It took her a couple of attempts to open it since her hands were shaking. Her mouth moved over words I didn't understand.

As soon as she had it open a little, I reached in and helped her push it up further.

She stepped back. "W-what are you doing?" she whispered.

Smirking, I placed my hands on the window ledge and pulled myself in.

"*What* are you doing?" she hurled in shock, her eyes rounded again.

"Comin' in," I replied with a chuckle.

She rolled her eyes at me. Biting her plump bottom lip, a frown tugged the edges down. "Jerimiah?" she whispered.

Planting my feet on the floor inside her bedroom, I stood. "So you do remember."

"What?" she asked, her hands clasping in front of her. She shifted from one foot to another. She was nervous to have me in her room. Ignoring her worry and trying to put her at ease, I dragged my gaze from her and glanced around in her room. With a name like Poppy, I expected her to be a girly-girl. But her room told me she was a mixture of that, and not. The bedspread was grey, her walls white, and she had posters ranging from Matchbox Twenty, to *Transformers* to…

Turning, I rose a brow. *"The Little Mermaid?"*

Her cheeks heated. "So?" she squeaked, which made her blush deepen. She focused on the floor, took a deep breath and then looked back up, glaring.

Cute.

"W-what did you mean? I do remember?"

"Me from school," I stated. After walking to the bed, I sat at the end, resting my hands behind me and watched her chest rise and fall rapidly. "Tell me why you were upset when you came in."

She spun away from my gaze and went to her desk. Pulling out a chair, she then stood for a moment more, fiddling with things on the desk. If she'd been any other girl, they'd have picked to sit next to me, hell, they'd have been thrilled to have me in their room, yet Poppy wasn't any other girl. I knew I was an okay-looking guy. I got enough attention from the opposite sex, so seeing Poppy act shy, pissed and annoyed with me being there, was nice.

She cleared her throat. "Like I'd said before, girl problems."

Rolling my eyes, I stated, "And that was a lie."

She huffed. "Okay then. It's none of your business." She crossed her arms over her chest and glowered at me like she wanted my head to explode.

Feisty. That was cute too.

Christ, I wished she hadn't crossed her arms though, because my eyes zoned in on her boobs, and they were pretty big for her age. I cringed and glanced around the room again. *I shouldn't be looking at her tits. Fourteen, man. Fourteen.*

"Right." I nodded.

She straightened, her brows dipping in confusion. "Right what?"

"Just decided we're going to be the fuckin' best of friends."

"No," she clipped, and when her face paled, it had me thinking whatever went down that night had something to do with Nicki. Bloody hell, I had to set that girl straight. She'd claimed me, but I was just havin' fun.

"Yes." I smiled. Least then, since we were friends, I could keep a better eye on her, and since she was Venom, it was my duty to make sure she stayed safe.

That was what I told myself anyway.

I stood and stalked towards her, got in her face, and smiled brighter. "See you at school, bestie."

"Jerimiah—"

Shaking my head, I flicked her nose. "Nope, no

getting' outta it now." I turned and went over to the window.

"Jerimiah," she called. Facing her, I watched her shift from one foot to another, and then added, "Um, we can, be like… friends, but no one can know about it at school."

Holy shit.

Any other girl would be ecstatic. Except Poppy.

With a wink, I said, "We'll see," and then slipped out the window.

CHAPTER FOUR

PRESENT

POPPY

*T*he murmured voices from the living room stopped so I knew Jerimiah had left. Standing from the floor, where I'd earlier slid after closing my door, I dressed quickly in jeans and a tee.

I knew I was being childish, with continuing my hate for Jerimiah, but he crushed my heart so many years ago, and seeing him rehashed the night I'd heard him talking about me.

God, I needed to get over it. I'd thought I hated him,

which helped me move away so easily, as well as the fact I did it to protect him.

Though, hate was such a strong word.

Honestly, I could never hate him when he'd been so important to me for so many years.

I was hurt. And I felt sick and guilty for never telling him the truth.

My hurt shone the brightest though. Hurt he never liked me more than a friend. Hurt my feelings had been nothing to him. So I kept telling myself I hated him, when in fact, I didn't. But still, I rode the hurt train even though I shouldn't.

Also, it was hard to face him when guilt threatened to consume me for never telling him everything.

Shopping, I deduced. It always put my mind at ease, and since I had a new waitressing job at a strip club, where the tips were amazing, I could afford to help Dad out *and* splurge on a few items. Turning to my desk, which was still decked out in my high school memorabilia, I reached to grab my bag. A shadow at the window caught my attention. Slowly, I moved my gaze there and tensed even more.

Fang.

My heart clenched behind my ribs.

Seeing him standing outside my window with a smirk was all too familiar. Like the time he'd first showed. I'd come home from the movies with Manda and unfortunately, I'd had a run in with Nicki. I shouldn't have let her cruel words get to me, but I'd been fourteen, and she'd been a huge bitch that night. Telling me all my faults in front of everyone, she'd laughed the loudest. I'd ran, fighting tears. Back then, I'd thought my life would never get better, until I'd seen a pair of dark brown eyes and a smiling mouth outside my window. It had been that night when Fang, who I'd called Jerimiah back then, promised me we were going to be friends from then on. We had. Only, as I requested, it was behind everyone's backs. At least for a while.

Stomping to the window, I unlocked it and pulled it up. "What?" I asked. My tone held a fraction of bite to it.

Ignoring me, he got close and lifted himself in through the window. Quickly, I moved back, which caused him to smirk. "We need to talk," he stated.

With a sigh, I ran a hand along the back of my neck and then dropped it, shaking my head. "We really don't. Besides, I was on my way out."

He straightened. God, he was so much taller than I was. Taller and hotter. Turning away, I went back to my desk and shifted a few things around to occupy myself and hoped if I ignored him enough, he would just leave. Jesus, I realised it was exactly what I'd done that first time.

"Poppy." His voice was low. "Why did you leave?" He

already knew a part of it, yet he was pushing at me to confess it all.

Shaking my head, I licked my dry lips and scoffed. "I guess, after talking to Dad, you know why I'm back."

"Yeah. I'm sorry to hear, darlin'."

I nodded once. "Can we just leave the past where it is?"

"No."

Grinding my teeth together, I faced him. "Just because you know what's going on with my mum doesn't mean I need you around. We're not friends, Fang—"

"Jerimiah," he bit out.

"What?"

"You've always called me Jerimiah. I was never Fang to you."

I glanced at the floor and shrugged. "Things change." When he stepped closer, I flicked my gaze up and scowled.

His voice lowered. "I didn't know you were there that night."

"It doesn't matter." We hadn't been anything back then but friends, and my emotions had been crushed after hearing him talk crap about me because I'd let myself fall for him. Yet, I was suddenly feeling foolish for the child-hood actions.

Actions that led me to behave like a bitch when I wasn't one.

God, I was pathetic. I wanted to hold onto my hurt, the pain, so I could distance myself from Jerimiah longer. I was worried that if we went back to the friendship we'd once had, my feelings would grow, and I wouldn't, *couldn't* hold back the other truth about why I left.

"D-do you speak with your father?" I found myself asking, and regretted it right away.

His face scrunched up in disgust. "No, and if I ever saw him, I would…. Fuck, let's just say it wouldn't be pretty."

Suddenly, I felt drained. Memories flashed through my mind.

PAST

Jerimiah's grin as he opened the door to me at his house was bright. It had been over a year since we'd become friends. He'd stuck to my rules, of being friends without anyone knowing, until today. I'd been sitting in the cafeteria with Manda, when Lennon, a guy from our class, came to our table and pulled out the chair next to me.

Glancing at Manda, I rolled my eyes, causing her to snort. She knew he was there to start something. He got off on picking on the less popular people.

"Tell me something, butch. Do the curtains match the drapes?"

Shifting, I leaned one arm on the table and the other

over the back of my chair, and then eyed his crotch before slowly looking up. "Tell me something, idiot. Does the brain match the balls?" I wasn't even sure it made sense, and it had sounded way cooler in my head. Still, from the dirty look Lennon sent me, he hadn't liked it, so it worked. Usually, I would sit back and say nothing since he'd been pretty mild in his taunts. However, earlier Manda told me how he'd tripped a grade seven girl over then pretended to lay over her and hump her, yelling about how much she enjoyed it. Of course, no teachers had been around, and when no one waded in to help her, Manda did, and she'd caught his attention from it, getting in her face and calling her everything he could think of at the time. Thankfully, Manda was a nut and didn't give a crap what he said. She barked back some things and got the girl away from him.

"That's just fucking stupid," he snarled.

"Sorry, I was just dumbing things down for you."

His face turned the same shade as my hair before his hand landed on my face, where he shoved me back with so much force, I landed on Manda's lap with a surprised cry. Just as I was about to raise my foot and kick him in the face, the room fell silent. All except for a chair crashing to the floor.

I watched as Lennon looked at where the noise had come from. His eyes widened before he scrambled to stand. I knew who was coming. Having spent so much time with him either at my place or at the compound with my dad, I could sense Jerimiah in a room full of people in seconds. Manda helped me sit, and then I thought it better to stand beside a terrified Lennon. Jerimiah was feared around the school. I just didn't realise how much.

"Wait, I—"

Jerimiah gripped the front of Lennon's tee and brought their faces close. "You think you can touch girls like that?"

"No, I didn't mean—"

"Bullshit. Whatever you're gonna say is bullshit."

Glancing around, I saw two of Jerimiah's mates making their way over to us. I also noticed a teacher was wading through the tables and chairs coming our way.

"Teacher coming," I warned.

Through clenched teeth, Jerimiah clipped, "You ever touch a girl like that again, *especially* Poppy, I will fuckin' take you down. You hear me?"

Lennon nodded.

"Apologise."

"Jerimiah Liang," the teacher yelled.

Lennon moved his gaze to me and muttered, "Sorry."

"It's fine." I nodded. Jerimiah didn't let up his glare or hold on the guy though. Stepping up, just as his friends arrived, I touched Jerimiah's arm. "Everything's fine. Come on, Jerimiah, sit down."

He took a breath and released Lennon as the teacher stepped up.

"What's going on here?"

"Nothing, just talking," Lennon spat out and then took off.

The teacher turned to me. "Poppy? Jerimiah? Manda? *Anyone* want to tell me what that was about?"

"For the life of me, I can't remember," I stated, and then smiled before sitting back down next to a stunned Manda.

"What she said," Jerimiah replied, and took the seat Lennon had vacated on my other side.

The teacher huffed, mumbled something under his breath, and stalked away.

Jerimiah's friends moved around the table and sat opposite us, looking just as shocked as Manda still was.

Jerimiah rested his arms on the table and turned just his head to face me. He was still scowling as his eyes ran over me, seeing if I was harmed in any way. Heck, it was only a hard shove, but he was acting like I'd been stabbed.

To lessen the tension, I grinned and then said, "Maybe next time you want to come to my rescue you could wear tights, briefs, and a cape. Like a real hero."

His gaze darkened for a second more until his lips twitched. Then he closed his eyes and sighed before gazing at me calmly. "Don't need to be a hero. It's what friends do for each other. Have their backs."

"So…," Manda started, until Jerimiah looked at her. She then squeaked and glanced everywhere else.

Laughing, I put her at ease. "Manda, Jerimiah. Jerimiah, this is my friend Manda. Oh, and Jerimiah conned me into being his friend too."

The guys across from us laughed. Jerimiah turned to them, and they quickly coughed to cover their humour.

"How?" Manda asked, finding her confidence.

"Our fathers are in the same motorcycle club."

Jerimiah's friend's faces brightened in understanding.

"Guess the cat's outta the bag now and you'll have to hang with us," Jerimiah said with a smirk.

"Ah, no."

I took a sip of my drink and heard Manda whisper, "Are you crazy?" while Jerimiah's friends' expressions went back to being shocked.

"Why?" Jerimiah pressed.

"You're in year ten. I'm in year eight. That should explain enough. If it's not, there's also the fact you annoy me too much."

Jerimiah chuckled, then ruffled my hair. "You adore me."

Rolling my eyes, I pushed his hand away. "You wish."

Since things were out in the open with us being friends, I decided to appear at his house that night because I'd only ever been there the once. However, it was only moments after arriving I wished I hadn't.

"What're you doin' here?" Jerimiah asked as he moved aside to let me in. Walking through, I stopped just to the side of the door so Jerimiah could close it. When he did, he took my hand. "Let's head to my room."

Then there was a bang at the back of the house, and I felt Jerimiah tense. We both looked towards the entryway and saw Jerimiah's dad stroll in.

"What are you doin' home?" Jerimiah asked gruffly.

Jerimiah's dad, who I knew as Switch, stopped and grinned. His eyes travelled over me slowly, and when he spotted my hand in his son's, he grinned. And it wasn't a nice one.

Ignoring his son, he said, "Charlie's girl, right? Poppy?"

"Yes, sir."

"Sir. Hmm, I like that." He winked before flicking his gaze to Jerimiah. "You two close?"

I was surprised when Jerimiah tugged my hand in his, and I teetered sideways. Jerimiah stepped in front of me. Like his father, he ignored that question, and asked, "What are you doin' home?"

Switch chuckled. I glanced over Jerimiah's shoulder and Switch met my stare.

It was then I saw it.

A gleam in his eyes. I didn't like it or trust it one bit. It felt wrong. *He* felt wrong.

CHAPTER FIVE

PRESENT

FANG

Talking of my dad dragged up too many hateful emotions. I needed Poppy to understand something else. "Poppy, I was seriously drunk outta my mind that night and talkin' shit. I didn't mean anything by it. Fuck, I'm sorry if it hurt you—"

She waved her hand out in front of herself. "It did a lot… because I'd been in love with you. But that was only part of why I left."

Shock locked my body in place.

She'd been in love with me?

Christ.

She'd *loved* me.

All the time I'd thought she'd seen me as an older brother. That night I'd been drunkenly wallowing in unrequited feelings I had for her and thought if I got some action in the sack, it'd take my mind off her. When I'd flirted with the woman who would take my mind off Poppy, the bird asked me about Poppy. I hadn't wanted to lose the chance to get off, so I'd lied and told her Poppy was nothing to me, nothing more than a nuisance who followed me everywhere. Fuck me. I'd even told her how I couldn't stand her attention... and Poppy had heard it all. She'd heard it and I'd crushed her.

She'd been in love with me like I had with her.

But... "Wait, what do you mean that was only part of why you left?"

She twitched, like her whole body spasmed.

"Poppy?"

"It doesn't matter." She snorted. "I seem to be saying that a lot." She shook her head. "But I've decided it really doesn't matter. I've just been stressed about, well, every-thing and..." She shrugged and smiled sadly. "I guess, I've been taking things out on you in a way."

"I'd still like to know."

Her jaw clenched. "Can we please just drop it?"

"Fuckin' hell, darlin'. You left me. We were close, and

you left without returning my calls and texts. It's gotta be aired about why you cut me out."

She fisted her hands at her sides. "Did you really care?"

"Of course I fuckin' did."

A snort. "If you did, if you really did, you would have taken the time to come find me."

Well… Christ.

I opened my mouth, then closed it.

Her brows rose and she smirked, as if to say, "See."

Throwing my hands up in the air in frustration, I explained my side. "You left me, Poppy. Like I meant nothing to you, and I didn't understand why. Fuck, I was hurting, confused, and goddamn pissed that the most important person in my life cut me out."

Pain flashed through her eyes. "I had my reasons."

"And I had mine why I didn't come to you. You know how stubborn I am. I got my back up about you leaving without a bloody word." I growled in the back of my throat. "But things change from now on."

Her head cocked to the side. "How?"

"We get back what we had, become friends again." And then, fuckin' then, I claim her in the way she'd never run from me again.

She straightened, a hand going to her stomach. It slid up over her heart and then stopped around her neck. "I-I don't know if I can."

"Why?"

"Fang—" She started but cut off when another frustrated growl rumbled up and out from my chest. With an eye-roll, she said, "Fine, Jerimiah." I nodded. "I need... my mum, work... I can't...." She let out her own cute, bitty growl. "My time's already busy."

"You'll fit time in for me."

She glared. "I don't know if I can."

"You will."

Another cute noise in the back of her throat followed. "You're still frustrating, demanding, and annoying."

Smirking, I winked. "And yet, you still like me."

Fuck. It was the wrong thing to say. The light in her eyes dimmed a little. I had to let things drop. For right then, I needed to leave things as they were, partly settled. But one day I'd find out everything I wanted to know.

To help her, save her, and make her mine.

Running a hand through my hair, I said, "Look, let's just see how things go, yeah?"

A deep breath through her nose made me grin as she said, "I suppose."

I chuckled. "I'm happy with that at least."

She nodded. "Um, I do have to go now though."

"All good. We'll catch up soon." She looked at me with scepticism. "Poppy, I'll be around. You can't get rid of me." She gave me another nod. "Would it be too much to hug it out?"

Her eyes narrowed. "Fa—erimiah."

"Poppy." I held my arms wide.

"No."

"Yes?"

"No," she demanded, though I saw her lips fighting to stay in their serious line.

"So... not yet." I winked. "We'll work up to it." I moved to the window.

"You can use the front door."

Turning, I shook my head. "This was how it was. This was us."

"Maybe we need change."

"No, babe. We had something good. I want it back, and I get what I want. You should know that by now."

"Jerimiah—"

"See you soon," I called, before smiling and climbing out the window.

Fuck me, but it felt like I walked back around to the front of the house with a new spring in my step. I'd left things too long, and honestly, I didn't know how much I'd missed my Poppy. Missed her in ways I'd blocked for a fucking long time. Hell, when we were close, I'd wanted her bad, but she'd been young. I'd planned on waiting until she was eighteen to claim her.... I'd fucked that up. Screwed it up royally by being the horny little fucker I'd been.

Then she'd left, and I drowned.

I'd sunk low without my Poppy around.

We'd get it back though.

We had to.

Swinging my leg over my ride, I couldn't help but think she was more stunning. She'd been stunningly cute back in the day, to a point I had to warn guys away from her.

My body stilled at a new thought. Did she have a guy already?

Shit. I wanted to go back to find out. I didn't. We'd left on a high, not at each other's throats, and I wanted it to stay that way for a while. Wanted to prove myself to her that I wasn't screwing us around.

A few hours later I was at the bar in the compound rolling my phone over and over in my hand while the other held a beer. Noise surrounded me, yet I didn't really hear what was going on. I'd already texted Charlie for his daughter's phone number, with a note I'd update him on his son when I found out his punishment. Since then, I tried to figure out a way to approach Poppy about if she had someone in her life.

Well, in a way that wouldn't piss her off. I couldn't really say, "Are you dating? If you are, get rid of him before I kill him." Or, "No guy had better be in your life because you're soon to be mine, and if there is, I'll kill him." Then there was, "You're mine, any guy touches you, I'll kill him."

I was starting to see a pattern in my ideas; they all ended in death. Just the thought of my Poppy being with someone else built a fuckin' furnace inside of me.

What I also noticed was that yeah, I'd been fuming about Nary and Vicious, but I'd never felt the furious heat I did with the thought of Poppy and another guy.

Guess it was because I'd always known something was gonna happen with Nary and Vicious. So when it did, I wasn't shocked by it. Yeah, it hurt I'd lost her, plus it killed she got taken on my watch, but I was finally content with knowing they were happy.

Fucking hell, I was even happy for the fucker Vicious.

"What's got your panties in a twist?"

Lifting my gaze from my phone, I watched Vicious taking the seat next to me. All happy thoughts for him vanished.

"Nothin'." I glared.

"How'd it go with the woman?" he asked.

My head jerked back a little in shock. I glanced around and then back to Vicious. "Are we really doin' this?"

"What?" He took the beer Gamer handed him and had a swig.

"Talkin' like we don't hate each other, like we're mates?"

"I don't hate you," he said, and then grinned. "I don't like you so much, but I don't hate you. Not since I got what I wanted. And we're brothers, so we gotta get along in some way."

"You know, Nary and I never slept together."

The bottle in his hand shattered, crumbled to pieces. He sneered. "We never speak of Nary and you ever again. Brother or not, I'll fuckin' slice your throat open."

Snorting, I smiled. Gamer looked at me like I'd lost my mind. "Right. So in my understanding, you don't want to talk about girly things, like how *your* woman is, and how *my* woman is."

His dark gaze swung my way, then lightened. "Fuckin' cocksucker."

With a laugh, I tipped my beer his way. He got me. I wasn't willing to talk about Poppy to him, and in return, I wouldn't talk about Nary.

Starr, Nurse's woman, popped up to the bar and rattled off an order for Gamer to fill. "Sweetheart, you do know the lazy motherfuckers here can come up and get their own drinks. This ain't Pick and Billy's pub," Gamer explained.

"Oh, I know, but I don't mind." She smiled, then glanced to Vicious and me. Her eyes slid down and then she yelled across the room, "My man... blood..." She gulped. "...Vicious. Blood."

"Shit," we heard Nurse curse. "Catch her."

Moving quickly, I pocketed my phone and wrapped my arm around her waist as her eyes fluttered in her head and her legs gave out from under her. Then she was dead weight in my arms. I lifted her, then carried her to a couch some brothers vacated for me and laid her down.

"Tell us again how you got a queasy one when you're known to work with blood day in and out, brother?" someone called.

"Fuck off," Nurse replied, heading to Vicious to fix up the cuts on his hand from the beer bottle. Chuckling, I left my brothers to watch over Starr, and made my way down the hall to my room.

Sinking to my bed, I lay back and again pulled out my phone. I sucked in a breath and opened up a text to Poppy.

Me: Tell me something I don't know about you.

Poppy: Who is this?

Me: Your friend.

Poppy: Sounds more like a creeper to me.

I chuckled. Her response reminded me of how she used to be around me: herself. She'd always said what she wanted without a care in the world. Well, eventually she had.

Me: Poppy!

Poppy: Yes, Creeper?

Me: I'll go by anything else other than creeper.

When I'd hit Send, I cursed my idiot self for leaving it wide open.

Poppy: Wanker? Clown? Sacklips? Any of those?

Me: Okay, bad move on my part. I'll ONLY go by Jerimiah or hot stuff.

Poppy: All right. Jerimiah it is. And to answer your question: I hate nachos.

What the fuck? She used to eat them all the time with me.

Me: Bull. You ate them with me.

Poppy: ....

Sitting, the realisation crashed into me once again. She only ate them *for* me, because she knew I fuckin' loved them. Hell, she had been in love with me. Only love would make a person suffer through a meal they hated.

Me: I'm not sure we can go on... not liking nachos is not human.

Poppy: Okay, it was nice knowing you again for the brief moment.

I frowned. The woman was too quick with that reply.

Me: I forgive you. I'm back in your life.

Fuck me. I'd sounded cheesy and desperate. Did I give a shit? Not one bit if I got Poppy where I wanted her. Liking me again, warming to me, smiling, laughing, and moaning.

Only there was no quick response from her end.

Me: Poppy?

Another minute later…

Me: Poppy!

Me: Goddamn it, babe. You're not getting away from me.

Poppy: Damn, it was good while it lasted. GTG :)

Me: Talk soon!

In the end, I realised I still hadn't found out the answer I wanted most. Was she involved with anyone?

CHAPTER SIX

POPPY

*T*hankfully, I'd been in my room getting ready for work when I'd got Jerimiah's text or else people would have seen the biggest, giddy smile and laugh I'd had in a while. At the time, I enjoyed being playful with him. We used to talk crap and give each other hell a lot, but then….

Rubbing my forehead, I placed my phone on the bed and picked up my short pink leather skirt and slipped it on. Confusion swirled in my mind. It wasn't that long ago I'd still hated him. Okay, not hate exactly, maybe hurt. But it was as if Jerimiah had magical powers and when I was in his presence, all I could think about was forgiveness, forgetting, and wanting him back in my life.

Shit. If I gave him what he wanted—my time—would I be back to where I'd left and in love with him even more? It was possible. He was more charming and sinfully hot. He had a way with words. Already I was considering taking hold of him and getting back to how we used to be. We spent a lot of our time hanging out, talking, sleeping over, taking care of each other, and confiding in one another.

I knew he'd hated his father with a passion, something I totally understood. But he loved his mother and stayed because of her. His favourite food was nachos, with a chocolate milkshake to wash them down. He loved all types of sports and had tried to teach me to play a few of them, until he realised my hand and eyes coordination wasn't good. That was after I was hit in the head for the fifth time from the basketball I was supposed to catch.

I knew he hated romance movies, but loved action. Typical guy. He'd also mentioned how he wanted more in life than what his father showed his mother. Since that wasn't much, I knew he could achieve it, and as far as I knew, he had. I'd heard how happy his mum was, especially when a few years ago, Switch, Jerimiah's dad, had left town without a trace and never came back. What I never expected was for Jerimiah to change motorcycle clubs. Venom had run through his veins. I never expected it, but I was glad he had. Back in the day, Jerimiah used to be broodier, unless he was around me, and even the few times I'd seen him since I'd got back to town, I'd noticed his change. He was a smiler. I could see he was happier. He'd freed himself from a MC that dealt on the wrong side of the law, and found a new family, one that supported one another, and was clean. Yes, I'd overheard of few times when the Hawks got dirty from being around Blackie and Dad, but the Hawks only ever did it because they were protecting their family. They protected in ways anyone hearing about it would understand.

I just didn't know them personally. *Not like I do with Venom MC.* They'd been a part of my family for a long time. Things were good with Blackie running the show. Dad was prouder now than he was when he'd first started out.

To me, Venom was family.

Which was why a part of me twinged when I learned Jerimiah had left the family.

We used to hang out at the compound, laughing at what the guys would get up to. Sneak a beer or two together, play pool, or just sit around on family days and eat all the food we could.

Sighing, I shook my head.

The past was the past.

I couldn't stop things changing, like I couldn't stop my mum getting sick.

We had to move with the flow. Deal with the pain and learn to grow from it all, no matter how much I wished to crumble under everything.

However, even though I would roll with everything, I couldn't bring myself to insert my life fully back into Jerimiah's. Not yet. I needed time and distance to see how things went. I was good with texts, but having him around, close, I found myself muddled.

Forgiveness was beautiful. I had forgiven him fully, of this I was now certain, but patience was also something to behold.

When my phone chimed again as I slipped the black tank top over my head, I smiled big again. Groaning at myself, I picked it up and opened the text… then dropped the phone.

Python.

After I'd been back in town a while, I'd visited the Venom compound one night and met Python. A big, tattooed guy around my age. He'd charmed his way in to get a couple of dates out of me. The first wasn't so bad. We hung out and talked at the compound, drinking, playing pool. But on the second date, I knew he wasn't for me. He had a look about him I didn't trust. He was rude to the wait staff, rude to the people at the bar, and in the end, when I wouldn't go home with him, he was rude to me.

I was called a cock tease, a bitch, a redheaded little fucker, and after all that, he'd tried to force himself on me. Thank God Dad had been home and came out to see what was going on. He hadn't seen what happened in the car, but didn't like how long we'd been out there without getting out. Python, knowing Dad was close with Blackie, backed off.

However, I didn't know what type of psycho he was until a few days later he'd texted me and told me how much he looked forward to finally claiming my pussy as his. Since I was already his woman.

That had been a few weeks earlier, and since then, I hadn't heard a word from him, so I thought he'd dropped the whole thing.

Until my recent text.

Psycho: Saw Hawks at your door. Don't fucking like it. You're mine. They come again, they pay.

If he was actually serious, I didn't know, and it scared me not knowing. When he hadn't done anything after threatening to fuck me, I thought he was full of shit. So when it came down to the crunch, I was already half convinced he was all talk and not an action man. If I showed Dad the texts, he'd freak, and he had enough to worry about. Still, if I didn't show him, he would be pissed. And if something happened to me, he would go crazy.

When I heard the front door open, I made a decision to tell him. Picking up my knee-high boots and handbag, I placed my phone in the latter then made my way out into the living room. He'd just sat down on his reclining chair with a long, loud sigh. He noticed me and managed a warm smile.

"You got work, honey?"

"Yeah." I smiled. "Until midnight."

"What time you start?" he asked, leaning forward to rest his elbows on his knees and then his head on his hands.

"In an hour."

"You got time for a chat?"

Shit. His voice didn't sound right. I knew whatever he had to say wasn't going to be good.

"Is it Mum?"

Pain slashed through his features, then regret. "No, honey. I'm sorry to get you worried. It's about your brother."

Letting out an annoyed grumble, I asked, "What's he done now?"

"Did Fang tell you anything?"

Raising my brows, I said, "No."

"Right." He nodded. "Sit down, honey. It won't take long." As soon as I was seated to his left on the couch, I dropped my boots on the floor, and he went on, "You know I'd sent him to the Hawks to see if that'd straighten him out."

"Yes. I guess it didn't." Alvin Torian was a pain in everyone's arse. He had never liked me. Heck, I wasn't sure if he liked anything or anyone. He stole, did drugs, got into fights, and on a few occasions, he threw parties that wrecked the family home. Those times Dad had kicked him out, but after a while, he'd beg to come back. His latest excuse was not coping with how things were with Mum. Only we knew it was never Mum. It was the drugs, and he was just a bad egg. Jerimiah even knew it. He beat the living crap out of him one night when Alvin had cornered me down the street asking for money. When I said I didn't have any, my brother attacked me, trying to steal my bag. That was until Jerimiah came around the corner. I'd been surprised when Dad told me Jerimiah was going to help Alvin transition into Hawks. What didn't shock me was Alvin messing the chance at a new life up.

"He was high, said some shit to a few Hawks members, and it didn't go down well. They taught him a lesson. He didn't learn from that because he then said some shit about *us* in front of Jerimiah. Fang lost it, and after he was done, he left him with his brothers to deal out more of a message. He's in the hospital, honey, and the shit he said about us…. I've cut him from our lives."

Shock had my lips parting and my body stiffening.

Dad had cut Alvin, his own son, from our lives.

Whatever had been said must have been serious. Deadly serious.

My father was smart, he cared a lot, and was the rock in the family. If he'd cut Alvin out, it was important to follow his lead. What helped was that letting Alvin rot in the hospital wasn't a great loss.

"If I see him, I'll let you know. He's no longer my brother."

He stood, reached down to grab my wrist, and pulled me up in front of him. Next, I was wrapped in his arms. "Been you and me for a long time, honey. Fuck, I'd be lost without you. So Goddamn lost. I tried. Tried so hard to save him in one way or another."

"Dad, don't. He couldn't be saved. This isn't on you, and it's not on Mum. It's no one's fault but his." Pulling back, I teared when I spotted wetness in my father's eyes. "We'll be fine. We always have been. Honestly, Dad, he hasn't been a part of this, us, a warm, loving family, for a very long time. He missed out. It was his choice to be who he wanted to be."

His bottom jaw wobbled a little. "He was my own son."

Pulling back, I said, "He was, but then he picked drugs over us. The Torian family is strong, loyal, smart, and loving. He stopped being a Torian when he stole right out of Mum's purse, when he punched you in the face after you caught him, and when he trashed the house you and Mum worked so hard for. We need to focus on Mum."

He sniffed, roughly wiped at his eyes, and tugged me in for another hug. "You're right. But promise me this, honey. I need you to live your life too. I got your mum, you know that, but—"

"Dad…" I stepped out of his arms and shook my head. "…let's just… I'm good. I'm fine in fact with how my life is."

"Fang—"

"No. I'm not talking to you about him."

"Thank fuck. Although, need you to know now, the crush you had on him when you were young, honey, it wasn't one-sided. That boy was taken with you as much as you were with him. I have a feeling he'll want to stick close to my girl, but if he ever fucks things up, I'll kill him."

"Dad." I groaned. "We're… I honestly don't know what Jerimiah and I are. What I do know is that I don't have time for any of this right now."

"That a girl. Make him work for it."

My mouth dropped open. Jesus Christ. Dad wanted Jerimiah and me together, as in a couple, not just friends. "I have no words for you right now. Dinner is in the fridge." I picked up my boots and put them on. After standing, I went to Dad, bent and kissed his forehead.

"Love you, girl."

"Love you more, Dad."

He scoffed. Smiling, I made my way out of the house and headed to work.

Charlie Torian hated the fact I worked at a strip club. If he had a choice, he'd take me each day and pick me up to make sure I was safe. The day I told him where my job was, I thought a little of him died inside. That gutted me. I knew he wanted the world for me. It took a while, but eventually, he understood what I wanted, and that was for my family to live comfortably. My earning helped in a lot of ways and meant Dad could spend more time with Mum, the love of his life. If I ever found that type of love, I knew Dad's dream for me would have come true. I would have found my world.

It wasn't until later at work I remembered I hadn't told him about Python, and I wasn't sure I could. He was going through enough. If I could just keep Jerimiah and his brothers away, maybe Python wouldn't do anything in the end. That was if he had actually been going to do something.

CHAPTER SEVEN

FANG

*M*e: Realised never asked where you worked.

It'd been a couple of weeks since I got Poppy back in my life without so much disdain attached to us. Since then, she'd dodged every chance I put out there to catch up face-to-face. It was driving me fuckin' insane.

It was night. I'd just finished late in the garage and was walking into the compound when my phone tinged.

Poppy: Is this you asking now?

Smiling, I shook my head, loving it when she was a smartass.

Me: Yes.

Poppy: At a day spa.

My brows dipped.

Me: But you work late hours.

I knew that because I'd tried to get her to come to dinner a few times at Ma's; she'd said she couldn't because of work. Then I reached out and tried lunch, her excuse was either housework, cooking or seeing her mum.

Poppy: It's called a day spa, but it actually does late hours. For all those people who work nine to five.

That didn't sit right with me. In fact, it reminded me of a TV show I'd sat through with Nary a few times. Fuck. For the life of me, I couldn't remember the name of it. At first, I'd hated the show, except one of the main characters was hot. Still, the gist of it was the woman had hit a rough patch, and the spa place she worked offered extra money if they jerked their clients off.

I halted.

Motherfucking hell. Was Poppy jerking guys off for money? I still hadn't gotten to the question if she was seeing anyone. She was good at deflecting any questions that were too personal, but I enjoyed the times we texted, so I let it slide until we were face-to-face. People could lie in texts. Not that I thought she would, but Poppy was still holding something back from me. I wanted to know what.

Me: You working tonight?

Poppy: No, heading in to see Mum.

Me: What are you doing tomorrow?

Jesus, I sounded desperate again.

Poppy: Banking, food shopping, and other boring things.

"Jerimiah?" I glanced up to see Nary coming my way.

"Hey, darlin'." I smiled. "What're you up to?"

"Nothing much really. I just popped in to see Low and then thought I haven't seen you in a long time, so I came to find you."

"Glad you did, babe." I wound my arm around her waist for a hug. Even though I'd lost Nary to Vicious, I was still glad we were close. We hadn't lost the friendship. Pulling back, I whistled. "Shit, woman, you're looking mighty fine. You heading out later?"

She giggled. "No, just came from work. Thought I might have a nice relaxing night."

"Yeah?"

"Yes, Sax—" She looked down at my phone, so I did, and we both saw the lit screen. Fuck. I'd called Poppy somehow as we were talking.

Placing it against my ear, I said, "Poppy?"

Silence for a beat, and then she said quietly, "You're busy. I'll let you go. Enjoy your relaxing night." Then there was nothing but air.

"Fuck!" I covered my eyes with my hand before slipping it up through my hair. I ran mine and Nary's conversation over in my mind. Shit. Poppy probably thought I was looking to relax with Nary.

"Was that the girl from the nightclub a while ago? The one Saxon said has your panties in a twist."

Scowling, I replied, "Remind me to hit your man in the face next time I see him."

"Uh, no. So it was her." She grinned, then her eyes widened. "Oh, our conversation may have been taken differently by her."

"Yeah, I reckon it did. Fucking hell."

Nary's hand came down on my arm. "I'm sure if you explain it to her, she'll understand."

Would she? Then again, should I explain myself when we were only at the friend stage? Yes, I fucking well should, because if it had been the other way around, I would be goddamn pissed. But was she... could she... hell, was there a chance for Poppy and me to be an us?

I think my balls just exploded from all the girl thoughts.

There wasn't a *chance* for us to be an us; it was a *fact* Poppy and I would be. I'd make sure of it. I'd fight her walls, smash them down, and make her see there was no one else for her but me.

"Gotta go make a call, babe. Talk soon, and give your man the middle finger for me." I grinned, even though I didn't feel like it, but it brought a giggle outta Nary, so I was glad. With a quick hug goodbye, I made my way through the compound to my room.

Sitting on my bed, I sighed and rolled my neck a few times. I pressed Poppy's name on my phone. It rang once before I got the message bank. I hung up, clenching my jaw. She was either on another call or she swiped across to end my call. I wasn't gonna have that.

Me: Call me or answer my next call or I'm coming to find you to talk.

I waited a few minutes, and when she didn't ring, I rang her again.

She answered, "Jerimiah, I don't have time to talk. Sorry, I have to—"

"Poppy, just give me five."

"I can't—"

"Please."

I heard her sigh. "Fine."

"I didn't realise I'd hit Call, but it happened, and what you heard was not what it was."

"Okay, not sure why you feel you have to tell me since it's none of my business, but okay. Now can I—"

"Jesus, Poppy. I wanted you to know because I want something to happen between us that isn't just friendship. You hear me?"

There was no response, but her breathing grew louder.

"Poppy?"

"I-I can't think about that now."

"I know, darlin'. It's too soon, but fuck me, I couldn't

have you thinkin' I was gonna go off and screw some bird. If it was the other way around, I know I wouldn't want anyone touching you."

"T-this, I… um…." She cleared her throat. I'd give my ride up if I found out what was going on in that head of hers. "She wasn't just some bird," she whispered.

"What?"

"She wasn't some bird. She was Nary."

"How do you know 'bout Nary?"

"I've heard things, and I've seen her, heard her voice down the street."

Fuck. I closed my eyes, breathed deeply through my nose, and asked, "What things you heard?"

"She was your woman when she got taken. Someone you love very much."

"You're right about one thing… she *was* my woman. She hasn't been for a fuckin' long time, but we're still close. What happened to her was fucked up in a big way. Never thought she'd find happiness again, and when I realised her happiness involved another guy, I stepped back. And that tells me I didn't love her all that much. If I did, I would have fought harder, and tried to get her to find her happiness with me."

Silence.

"Poppy?"

"I don't know what to say," she confessed quietly.

"Then don't say anything. I'll let you go, but before I

do, I need you to understand I lost the one woman I thought could be *my* happiness, *my* forever. I lost her, but now she's back, and I want to see where we could take it to gain back what we had. Only more." I paused to see if she'd say anything. When she didn't, I finished with, "Think about what I said, Poppy. One day, maybe you can see something special with us and want to reach for it. I'm not losing you again."

Hanging up, I lay back on the bed and cursed myself. Christ, if I just fucked everything up by saying shit too soon, I'd forever regret it.

I could only pray I hadn't word vomited our soon-to-be relationship down the drain.

POPPY

My chest ached because I'd stopped breathing. Clutching my phone to my stomach, I dragged in the oxygen I needed, only it was unsteady. Shaky. Just like my body. My mind was rambled with so many thoughts. At first, when I'd heard Nary and Jerimiah talking, it hurt. No, it crushed me.

Since the phone call, I didn't know what to think because my mind was stuck on one thing.

Jerimiah wanted a relationship with me.

Me. Poppy Torian.

Did he seriously just state he thought I was his forever?

What did I do with that information?

What do I do?

Shit. God. It was too soon, and I still hadn't told him the other reason why I'd left. He also didn't know I worked in a strip club. I was pretty sure I dodged a bullet with my lie, though I wasn't sure why I lied. All right, that was bull. He'd hate it more than Dad.

Then there was the whole Python thing.

The douche hadn't text again. Although I'd been getting the feeling of being watched. It was a freaky feeling, one that caused my hands to shake and the hairs on the back of my neck to rise. Then again, I could have been just paranoid, letting my mind run, more than it should.

"Poppy?"

My body jolted. I spun around in the kitchen to face Dad. "Sorry, what?"

He studied me for a second, then crossed his arms over his chest. "What's wrong?"

I snorted, "Nothing," then shifted back around to the counter where I had been preparing popcorn with melted caramel sauce for our movie night.

"Poppy, who was on the phone?"

"No one."

"Honey," Dad clipped, using his authoritative tone.

Sighing, I finished drizzling the sauce over the popcorn and turned with the bowl in my hand. "Let's finish this movie."

"I swear to God if you don't—"

"It was Jerimiah," I blurted.

"He the one you been texting lately?"

Narrowing my eyes, I sent him a glare before moving around him in the doorway and heading back into the living room. I sat on the couch while Dad walked in and took his place in his chair.

I waited. A few seconds later, he asked, "Do I have to hunt him down and cut him up?"

With an eye-roll, I smiled. "No." And then I shoved a mouthful of popcorn in.

"Been watching you the last couple of weeks with your phone. You're always on it, and smiling in a way that I knew it wasn't your girl, Manda. Haven't seen you smile like that in a long time, honey. But then when I walked into the kitchen, I saw a look of... fuck, I don't know, fear in a way. Your old man's worried, honey."

He knew where to hit me to get what he wanted. I hated the thought of Dad worried and if I could stop it from happening, I would.

Absently, I flicked a few kernels around in the bowl, and said, "He wants... Jerimiah wants to date me." When Dad said nothing for a while, I glanced up to find him beaming at me. "What's that look about?" I demanded.

"He's making his play. Halle-fuckin'-lujah."

"Dad!"

"What?" He shrugged. "Told you that boy was smitten back in the day, and I knew he still was when he came here a few weeks back. 'Bout time he confessed it."

"You shouldn't be saying that. Normal dads would warn their daughter away from a guy like Jerimiah. Normal dads would threaten him with a shotgun."

He scoffed. "Please. This normal dad knows when he sees something good for his daughter. Someone I know will protect her with his whole body and soul. He'd do anything for you, honey. Always has. If you ask me, it's you who should be worried. If he finds out where you work, and somehow sees all those dudes talkin' to you, lookin' at you—" He whistled long and loud. "Remember when you went on your first date?"

Groaning, I rested my head back on the couch. "Yes," I hissed.

Dad chuckled. "Yeah, I see you're gettin' it. Now pass the popcorn and just roll with whatever happens."

I wasn't sure if I could roll with it. First, I had to do something about Python. Maybe my best shot talking to Blackie. Then maybe, just maybe, I could actually acknowledge the brewing feelings inside of me for Jerimiah. He'd wormed his way in with every text in the last few weeks. Hell, Dad had certainly given Jerimiah the seal of approval. Though, he'd already given it years ago —the night Jerimiah brought me home after my first failed date. It was also the night I fell in love with Jerimiah.

CHAPTER EIGHT

PAST

POPPY

*T*oby and I had just stepped outside the burger place when he took my hand. I was waiting for the butterflies to happen, to start fluttering in my belly in excitement, but they must have been dead or maybe just asleep.

Instead, I felt grossed-out because Toby's hand was sweaty. Though, Manda did warn me boys sweated a lot when they were nervous. So maybe Toby *was* nervous. About what I didn't know. We'd already gone for a walk in the park and eaten dinner while we tried to find things to talk about. The date was nearly done.

God… was Toby thinking about kissing me? Was that why he was nervous?

I didn't want Toby to kiss me. Not unless those butterflies woke the hell up and went haywire inside of me. Then at least I'd know I had some type of feeling for Toby, other than boredom.

When Toby had asked me out the other day in the library, I was shocked. After all, I'd been at school for just over two years and he'd never shown any interest in me before. Still, he'd spoken to me with confidence—confidence he failed to have on the date night—and asked me out in front of Manda. Since it took courage for him to do it, and in front of a friend of mine, I said yes. After all, he was cute. There was also the fact Nicky had had her eyes set on him, but he'd asked *me* out.

Thankfully, Nicky was no longer on Jerimiah's radar, and hadn't been for a very long time. She hated me for it, blamed me for it. But it wasn't me who got caught talking shit. Nicky had been in my face telling me how she was going to ruin me, that Jerimiah was only pretending to be my friend because of the club our fathers were in. How he felt obligated to look after me. The look on her face—when Jerimiah appeared out of nowhere, and had heard everything, then proceeded to tell her to fuck off, and if she ever breathed our air again, she would regret it—was the best moment of my life.

It was later, when Jerimiah snuck into my room once again, he'd told me what Nicky said was all bullshit. I'd rolled my eyes and shoved him, replying with how I knew that already. I was too awesome not to love. Of course, he chuckled, something I loved to make him do, especially when his whole face changed, and all his hate for his father disappeared.

"What time do you have to get home?" Toby asked, dragging me from my thoughts. Jerimiah seemed to consume my mind a lot, and I knew I was falling for him more and more each and every day. I'd never actually admit I already loved him, because it was wrong. He was my friend, and also, he'd never see me as anything else. How Jerimiah still dated… okay, hooked up around me was proof enough for that.

"Ah, anytime really. My parents think I'm at Manda's."

Shit. I'd said it without really thinking and wished I hadn't. I'd been stopping myself from eye-rolling and yawning all night and had just lost my chance to get the hell out of Dodge. Maybe I could fake a period. Jerimiah hated when I talked about being on the rag. He even paled a few times. *Hmm, maybe I should stop if I was ever going to impress him.* Laughing under my breath, I knew the day I impressed Jerimiah into liking me more than a friend would be the day I aced all my classes. As in never.

Toby gave me a strange look.

Stop thinking about Jerimiah and laughing for no reason.
You look crazy.

"Really? So any time then." He smiled, looking down at me. Of course he was taller, most guys were. But I found myself not liking his smile.

"Y-yes. Do you want to see a movie?" Since being around Jerimiah so much, my confidence had grown. I'd stopped thinking about what other people thought about me.

"No." He shook his head. Then with his hand still in mine, he pulled me down the alley beside the burger place.

When my back hit the wall and Toby moved in to kiss me, I placed my hand on his chest and pushed him back. "What are you doing?"

"Kissing you, silly. Come on." He took hold of my wrists and tugged them down from his chest so he could lean in again. When his mouth touched mine, I wanted to kick him in the balls. There was a lot of spit as he tried to pry my mouth open with his tongue.

"Get off," I mumbled, because there was no way I was opening my mouth all the way. I struggled to get my grip free so I could punch him in the face.

He lifted his head and glared down at me. His shy boy act disappeared; instead, there was nothing but jerk before me. "Relax and enjoy it," he told me. "Shit, you give it up for Fang, why not me?"

My body stilled. Then I twisted my wrists from his grip, which kind of hurt, and placed them back on his chest, shoving and saying, "Jerimiah and I are *just* friends."

He scoffed, not moving away from me at all. "Yeah right. He'd have to hang out with you for a reason. You totally have to be putting out for him, and your pussy must be heaven for him to keep coming back."

Screwing up my face, I yelled, "You sick dick." Kicking out, I planted my foot into his shin, then lifted my leg and kneed him in his balls.

Toby stumbled back, cursing me. "Fuck Nicky. I ain't putting up with you." He started down the alleyway.

"Wait." I grabbed his arm. "What do you mean Nicky?"

He sighed, turned and said, "Nicky said if I wanted a piece of her, I had to get you out on a date and see if you put out for me. Look, I didn't want to, but then my friends heard about it and got me to agree. She told me what to say if you said no, and if I did get in your pants, she wanted proof." He pulled his phone from his pocket and hit End. He'd been taping the whole thing. "She'd… let's just say I'd have a happy ending if it all happened like she wanted it to."

A car out front screeched into the car park. We heard the door opening before it was slammed closed.

Pounding footsteps hit the stairs up to the burger joint, then the bell sang. Toby and I glanced at each other.

"Who do you—" I began.

"*Where in the fuck is she?*" was bellowed from inside.

"Oh fuck," Toby whispered.

Oh fuck was about right. Jerimiah had just arrived, and he was pissed.

A clatter of something more from inside, then raised voices answered, and then... the tingle of the bell sounded again. It had Toby backing up and shoving me in front of him.

"I only tried to kiss you. I didn't try anything else. You kicked me in the balls and I was just going to walk away. Tell him that."

That was true. Not many guys would have put up with being kicked in the balls.

With the street light facing down at the end of the alley, it lit Jerimiah's form as it appeared in the entry-way. His legs were apart, his arms down at his sides, his hands clenching and unclenching. His face... I had never seen it so dark before. If I didn't know him, know we were close, I would have been scared out of my mind.

"Poppy. Come here," he snarled.

"Um, I don't think so." I crossed my arms over my chest.

"Poppy," he growled. "Here. Now."

"You know, I don't think I will until you promise not to harm Toby."

"Thank you," Toby whispered behind me. His voice held a little awe, probably surprised with how I conversed with Jerimiah.

Jerimiah let loose a rumbled growl from within his chest. His eyes flashed from me to Toby, and I actually gulped. That look was pure pain. Pain he wanted to deliver on Toby.

His chest heaved and he rolled his head side to side a few times before saying, "Saw Nicky at a party. She wanted a piece of me. When I said no, she got pissed, and you know what she told me?"

When Toby didn't answer, probably from fear, which was wise, I did, "That she's really the Wicked Witch of the West?"

"No." He started down the alley very slowly. "She told me how she set that motherfucker up to take you on a date. Said he was gonna fuck you over because my little pet didn't deserve me. She told me how much better she is than Poppy. So you know what I said to her and every-fuckin'-one else at the party?"

"That you're going to turn into the Hulk and smash."

Toby snorted at my back, and it was the wrong move. Jerimiah's eyes slammed to him. "No," he growled. "I told Nicky to get the fuck outta my face before I forgot she was a girl and kicked her arse. She didn't move. I then told the room if they were smart, they'd cut Nicky from their life. Cut her out of all social groups or they'd have *me* to deal with. Then, fuckin' then, I said if anyone was to screw with Poppy again, in any way, I would make them pay tenfold. After that, I left because I had a cunt to hunt down and kill. Can you guess who that cunt is?"

When he finished, he stopped just in front of me.

"Jerimiah, there will be no killing tonight. I will not be visiting my best friend in jail. Besides, Toby's cool. After I kicked him in the balls, he was about to leave when you turned up."

His eyes knifed down to me. "Why'd you kick him in the balls, Poppy?"

Shit.

"Ah...."

In a flash, he reached around me and had Toby by the neck. Frantically, I gripped Jerimiah's arm and begged, "Let him go. Jerimiah, I swear it, if you don't let him go, I'll... Goddammit, I'll never talk to you again."

Jerimiah didn't listen. Gently, he shoved me out of the way and took the steps needed to have a struggling Toby against the wall, and then he was up in his face. "You think to touch her in any way again, I will bury you alive."

"I won't," was what I thought Toby gurgled out.

Wrapping my arms around Jerimiah's chest, I tugged

him back. Only he didn't move at all. "Jerimiah, he didn't do anything. Just let him go. Please."

Toby was dropped. He coughed, wheezed and then dry-heaved. Bet he'd never been so scared in his life. Jerimiah had that type of effect on people.

"Go. Get the fuck outta my sight."

Toby nodded, shot me a grateful glance, and then bolted for the end of the alley. Jerimiah still had his back to me. I stepped away from him, crossed my arms over my chest and waited to have his eyes. Once he turned, I raised my brows.

"Don't," he ordered. "Get in my car, Poppy."

"Seriously? I had everything under control, Jerimiah. That poor guy just about peed himself, and it wasn't even his fault. It was Nicky's. When he got the message of my knee in his balls after one kiss he… s-stopped."

I had to learn to not divulge everything to Jerimiah.

"He kissed you?" he roared. "Force himself on you? That's why you kicked him in the nuts?" He stomped off back down the alleyway, no doubt visualising the ways he would kill Toby.

But really… "You're overreacting," I mentioned from behind him.

He spun around so fast it made *me* dizzy and got in my face so our noses touched. "I'm overreacting to my friend, *my* best fuckin' friend, being touched without wanting it?"

"Who said I didn't want it?"

"What?" he barked.

Looking into his eyes, I said, "I'm a single girl. I'd like to try dating and see where things lead. As for my first kiss, it was a little sloppy, but still okay." That was a lie. "I may even try it again."

"You... I... fucking hell. If you want Toby to live, stay the fuck away from him."

"I didn't say it would be Toby."

"No," he bit out.

"No?"

His eyes heated. "No dating, Poppy."

"Why do you get a life and I don't?"

"It's different. I'm older. Shit. I'm not discussing this with you." He straightened, took my arm and led me to his car.

On the drive back to my place, I was fuming. Jerkface Jerimiah had double standards. Hell, he was dating when he'd just turned fifteen, he'd told me so one night, and *I* was nearly sixteen goddamn it.

A new thought dawned on me. After Jerimiah's display of protectiveness in the alley, and at the party... "No guy will be brave enough to date me again. I'm going to be a virgin for the rest of my life."

Beside me, Jerimiah coughed, growled, and then snapped, "Do not talk about being a virgin, sex, or guys in front of me at all. Ever."

Pulling into my drive, he got out, came around to my side and tugged me from the car. Moping, since my love life was doomed, and there was no way I would get over Jerimiah if I didn't find someone else, we made our way to the door. When Jerimiah didn't enter right away—instead he knocked—I knew he was going to be a pain in my arse.

The door opened and in it stood Dad. "Fang? What's—"

At the time, I'd been hiding off to the side of the door, until Jerimiah pulled me into view.

Shock ran over Dad's face. "Poppy? I thought you were at Manda's."

"Um, about that," I said with a nervous laugh.

Dad crossed his arms and glared. "What did you do?"

Jerimiah cleared his throat. "She wasn't at Manda's, Charlie. She decided to go on a date with a dickwad of a guy. Things could have gone bad if I hadn't shown—"

I snorted. "I had it under control before you showed up like a gym junkie on 'roids, or better yet, a rabid Rottweiler." I glanced at Dad, and I was sure I saw his lips twitching before he thinned them. I explained, "The guy kissed me. I didn't like it, so my knee made out with his balls."

Dad choked. He cleared his throat and opened his mouth to say something, but Jerimiah got in there first. "She's too young to date—"

"You did not just say that," I screeched, turning to him.

He faced me and glared. "I did. Get over it. You're fifteen. You shouldn't be thinking about dating. If I hear about you sneaking out of this house"—I opened my mouth, but his hand came up and covered it—"or Manda's, I will find you, sit down with you and your date, and make sure he *does* piss himself in front of you. That should put you off dating for a while."

Groaning, I grabbed his hand from my mouth and then shoved him in the chest. The jerk didn't move. I fumed. "You have got to be kidding me? You double-stan-dard prick." I threw my hands up in the air before stomping inside. Thankfully, Dad moved out of the way. Turning back, I gripped the door, and said, "I'm sure you have nothing to worry about anyway, Jerimiah. No guy would want to date me because they're too scared of you." I wanted to slap the smug look off his face.

"I'll lift the ban when you're eighteen," he stated, like he was doing me a favour.

A bubble of laughter came from my father. I glared at him, then at Jerimiah. "Do. Not. Talk. To. Me. For... at least a week. I don't want to see your face, you've pissed me off that much."

"Poppy," he said softly.

"No!" I yelled, and then slammed the door in his face. Sighing, I rubbed my temples because I had a huge headache. I asked Dad, "Am I in trouble?"

His hand came to my back and he ran it up and down in a soothing motion. "Nah. Besides, I reckon I don't have anything to worry about with you and dating. Fang has it covered."

Grumbling under my breath, I stormed off to my room. Opening my door, I wasn't at all surprised to find Jerimiah sitting on the end of my bed.

As I closed the door and locked it, I felt Jerimiah stand. Ignoring him, I went to my bed grabbed my night-wear and started taking off my clothes to put them on. Glancing at Jerimiah, I saw I had his back, like every time I did this. I pulled back my cover and got into bed, leaving the light on for Jerimiah to turn off before he left. If he thought he could stay, he had to rethink it.

"Poppy," he sighed out my name.

"Go away, Jerimiah."

"No." My body bounced as he landed on the bed to lay next to me. "I'm sorry, okay. I may have gone a little crazy."

I snorted. "A little?"

"A lot then. But when Nicky said she set that dick up to date you, and… I lost it. I hated the thought of anything happening to you."

Exhaling through my nose, I rolled to my back and looked up at him. My bottom lip suddenly trembled.

"Poppy." He groaned like he was in pain.

"Don't you realise what it all meant in the end? No

one will date me if someone hasn't set them up in the first place. I'm the unlikeable… undesirable."

He grabbed my hand. "Bullshit." With his other hand, he tucked a strand of hair behind my ear, and when his fingers brushed my cheek, the butterflies woke. *Now you want to wake up. Go the hell back to sleep.* Jerimiah caught my chin between his fingers. "You're liked, desired. Shit, I've lost count of the times my friends have asked me if they could take you on a date."

My eyes widened. "Seriously?"

Rolling his eyes, he nodded. "But I don't want you to rush into anything. You're my girl, you deserve the best, and the idiots I know aren't that."

My heart stopped.

His eyes, his beautiful eyes shifted, and they'd shifted down to my lips and then back up to my eyes. My heart thumped hard. Then it took off in a leap. The goddamn butterflies fluttered around inside me like they were on Red Bull.

"Just… fuck, wait for a bit longer, 'kay?"

All I could do was nod, because it was then, right then, in that moment I admitted to myself I was one hundred percent in love with my best friend.

"Let's get some sleep." He got off the bed, turned off the light, and I knew he'd be losing his tee to the floor, sometimes even his jeans, which left him in his boxers. At the thought of his godlike body, I got a funny feeling down below, as in, *below*.

He climbed into bed, pulled me close and ordered, "Go to sleep."

And because I didn't want to ruin us, even when I found myself fighting with my emotions to want to jump him and kiss him, I didn't. Instead, I said, "You go to sleep."

He chuckled. "Poppy."

"Jerimiah."

"Jesus."

I smiled into the night. I wasn't sure who won the fight, but I felt great. I felt so great because I had my best friend beside me. A friend I loved with everything I had. As I lay there in the dark room, I promised myself that one day, I would have the courage to see if there was ever a chance Jerimiah and I could be more.

CHAPTER NINE

PRESENT

FANG

"Come to the bar with me. The brothers are having a welcome back thing for Dallas's woman and her friend," I said into the phone a few weeks later to Poppy. She'd managed to dodge me every chance she got. I was sure some of the reasons for it was because she was freaked about my declaration, but I had a feeling there was something else holding her back from seeing me in person, maybe the other reason she'd left me in the first place. Didn't stop us from calling and texting though, and that was the only thing keeping me from losing it.

Nearly a month without sight of her was fucking eating at me.

I'd tried. Fuck had I tried. Randomly I'd show at her house to see if she was there. She hadn't been. Charlie thought the runaround was hilarious, especially when he saw how frustrated I got. It was good to see him happier those times I popped in. Mary was a little healthier since she wasn't refusing to eat anymore. What also helped Charlie, I reckon, was knowing Alvin had been set up in a place out of town, a rehab to get clean, and I told him if that didn't help, we'd figure something else out. The family was going through enough. No way would I let a drugged-out son and sibling darken their steps again. Unless he got his act together, but I doubted it.

"Jerimiah, I can't. I have work." I heard a knock on her door in the background. She muttered a curse before saying, "I have to go. Someone's at the door."

"I'll wait."

"Jerimiah—"

"I'll wait, Poppy."

She sighed, and I smiled. I heard her shuffling, the door being opened, and then Muff's voice. "Yo, towel lady." A pause, then, "Wait, don't I know you from some-where?" Another pause, before Muff added, "Can't remember. Anyway, just droppin' this off for my brother."

I'd paid Muff to drop off a burger from her favourite joint along with flowers and some chocolates. If I wanted to win her, I knew she'd love that shit.

"Jerimiah," she whispered into the phone.

Grinning, I said, "Eat, relax before work, and we'll talk real soon."

"Thank you."

"You're welcome, Poppy. Is Muff still there?"

"Yes."

"Tell him to fuck off."

Her laugh warmed my soul. "I will."

Yeah, one way or another, I would have my Poppy in front of me, in my arms, and warming my bed.

POPPY

I knew my feet would be dragging at work that night. I was already so tired from being up half the night talking to Manda about everything going on. Of course she was Team Jerimiah, always had been, even after I told her what he'd said that night. She'd believed there was an excuse for it. At the time of my leaving, she hadn't known about the other reason, until recently. She was upset I kept it from her, but had understood. Well, eventually.

Earlier, I'd texted her about the kind gesture Jerimiah had done.

Manda: OMG, jump him already.

Then my phone had rang.

"Hey." I'd smiled.

"Hey, yourself. Girl, please tell me you're on your way to see how well-hung Jerimiah is."

Laughing, I'd shaken my head, and said, "No."

"Damn. Okay, since you don't have any good news, I have some for you."

"What?"

"I just found out before…. I'm moving back to Caroline Springs. I got a job lined up already."

My breath had caught as tears filled my eyes.

"Honey?" Manda had whispered.

"I'll have you back," I'd mumbled.

"Yeah, and I'll have you back."

My chest had swollen, my emotions too much. "I'm so excited, Manda," I'd then yelled, before laughing.

She'd giggled along with me. "So am I, honey. So am I."

My body jolted. Thoughts of the call trickled away when Dad asked, "You want me to come in?" He sat in the driver's side of his car; mine had chosen to die just before work. Dad offered to give me a lift, which I'd had to accept. I hated him taking me, as every time he saw where I worked, it worried him.

"No, I'm good. Thanks for the lift. I'll see you at midnight."

His lips thinned. "You know you should tell Fang where you work."

"Yes, Dad. I will soon." *Maybe.* Leaning over, I kissed his cheek. "Don't worry about me. You know there are bouncers everywhere inside. I'll be fine."

He grunted.

"Dad—"

"Let your old man worry, okay?"

Smiling sadly, I nodded. "All right. See you later," I said, then climbed out of the car.

Jimmy, the bouncer at the front door, gave me a huge smile and let me through the gated-off front entrance. Dad had refused to take me around the back where I usually entered; he said it was too darkly lit. To ease his mind, I didn't argue.

Quickly, I went out the back to store my bag and jacket, then slipped out the front and straight to the bar. William, one of the barmen, grinned. "Just making up table eleven's order, Poppy."

"Thanks, Will." I winked.

"What. The. Fuck." I heard behind me.

With my heart in my throat, I slowly turned to find Muff, Jerimiah's brother who I'd just met officially that afternoon. Shit. Damn. Suck on some dirty balls. My mouth opened and closed again and again.

"Bloody knew I knew you from somewhere. You work here."

"Muff—"

"Does my brother know?"

"Shh," I muttered, and stepped closer to Muff, my gaze flicking around the busy room. "He doesn't *yet*. But I plan on telling him."

He whistled. "Babe, you are fucked. Can I be around when you tell him?"

"Everything okay here, Poppy?"

Glancing to the side, I nodded to Dale, another bouncer. "It's fine."

"Yeah, dickhead. It's fine."

"Muff!" I snapped.

He didn't look at me; he kept his eyes on Dale. "What? He knows who I am, the club I belong to. So he knows I'm here for extra security since this is a Hawks MC business. He's come up just to piss me off."

Hawks MC business?

How did I not know Hawks owned this club?

I'd always guessed the manager, a man in his forties, who looked like a Greek god, had owned it.

But he didn't.

It was Hawks.

Jesus. No wonder I'd seen members of Hawks in and out all the time. I'd just thought it was a club they frequented at, while I also prayed none of them took notice of me.

"You lot walk around here like you own the joint—"

Muff stepped closer to Dale. I grabbed his arm. "News flash, dickface. We *do* own the joint. What part of this place is a Hawks MC business did you not understand? Run along and do your job."

"Dale" was called. Glancing to the left, Samuel, the manager of the club, stepped up to Muff and Dale's side. "Get the fuck back to work."

Dale shifted his hard gaze to Samuel, then stormed back to his spot beside the stage.

"Sorry about that," Samuel offered.

"That guy needs to check his attitude to the club members. I ain't the only one he's tried to start shit with," Muff said.

"I know. I've been watching him. He's ex-cop, doesn't understand how Hawks runs things differently to other clubs."

Muff snorted. "Sammy, he'd better get the picture soon, or he'll regret it and come up to the wrong brother."

"I'll have another word with him." Samuel nodded.

"Poppy," William called. He lifted the tray, and I nodded.

"I have to work," I said to Muff.

"I'll be keeping an eye, babe."

"Is there something I should know?" Samuel asked.

"No!" I cried at the same time Muff replied, "Yes. She's a brother's woman."

"I am not," I demanded.

Muff snorted. Ignoring them, I huffed, glared, and then turned my back and got started on delivery drinks to my tables. I also ignored the pleasure that shot through me when Muff said I was Jerimiah's woman.

IT WAS NEARING 11:00 p.m. I'd just placed some drinks on a table and moved away when I felt heat at my back. A steel arm folded around my chest while something pressed into my lower spine.

"Shut up" was snarled low into my ear. Python. "Didn't like your job, but especially don't like my bitch flaunting herself for Hawks motherfuckers. Saw you out there flirting with him. Been watchin' him watch you. I don't fuckin' like it. If you make a sound, I'll shoot everyone I can before they help you."

I nodded. With trembling hands, I placed my tray on a nearby speaker. There was no way I would cause a scene and risk other people's lives.

"See I'm gonna need to teach my bitch a lesson, as well as Hawks. Now back the fuck up."

Shit, shit, shit. He was leading me towards the back

hall. If he got me down there and then out the back door, I wouldn't last the night. Fear ate at me, tears threatened to spill over, and my hands shook even more as I reached them up to hold his arm around my chest to keep up with him.

Only his pace was too fast. I stumbled. His grip on me tightened, but not enough and I landed on my arse. He bent, backhanded me and I fell to the side. Apparently, that wasn't enough for him. His hand fisted my hair. When I cried out, he backhanded me again.

Dizziness overtook me. My sight darkened until I blinked again and again. I couldn't pass out.

"Hey" was shouted a few paces away.

"Fuck," Python barked. He straightened and fired off a shot. I heard a curse and knew he'd hit someone. Scared, not only for myself but others, I kicked out over and over with both feet towards his legs. He tried to grab for me, to jump over my legs, but I connected a few times to make him trip. He stepped back again and again, as more male shouts sounded at the end of the hall before bullets were launched. Python ducked and weaved. He sneered down at me before he fired back and shifted out the back door.

Why hadn't he trained that gun on me?

He had a chance. Why didn't he shoot at me?

"Poppy!"

It didn't make sense.

Did he really want me with him so much he wouldn't kill me? Did he truly believe he'd claimed me? Confusion rolled around in my mind.

Someone shook my shoulders. I blinked up at Muff hovering over me. "Jesus, woman. You okay?"

I nodded, even though my head was throbbing. I placed my hands behind me and slowly, with Muff's help, I sat, leaning against the wall. Blinking again, I noticed blood dripping down Muff's arm.

I gasped, reaching for him. "You're bleeding."

Muff took my hands in his. "Relax, babe. It's fine. I'm good."

People crowded around us, some swearing, some on the phone, others talking, but all I could do was watch the blood drip down Muff's arm.

"Poppy," Muff called.

Dragging my eyes up to meet his, he grinned. "Come on, let's get you up. You're flashin' your panties, and I know my brother would kick everyone's arse if he knew other men could see them."

Glancing down, I realised my skirt had risen up high. After everything, I didn't expect I'd blush over it. With a nod, I caught Muff's hand as he stood and helped me to my feet. I swayed a little. Muff placed his hands on my shoulders.

"He made you bleed," I mumbled.

"Yeah, babe. He'll pay for that and markin' you."

"Jerimiah's going to be so pissed."

Muff snorted. "Babe, I'm thinking he'll be a bit more than pissed."

Shit.

ABOUT TWENTY MINUTES LATER, the club had been closed, and I was standing at the bar icing my face, under Muff's instructions, when I felt it.

The type of fury so fierce it choked the room.

It was so thick men parted for the one it was pulsating from.

Then I saw him.

Jerimiah strode through the room with his body rigid, his face tight in anger, no… rage, and he was headed right for me.

I wasn't scared. Not for myself at least. But if anyone around us said the wrong thing, I knew he would lose the control he held. He was hanging on by a thread.

He stopped right in front of me and bent so our noses touched. His voice low, grumbly, he growled the words, "You work in a strip club."

"Ah, at least I don't dance."

His jaw clenched. His eye twitched. "You work in a motherfuckin' strip club," he roared in my face.

"Not sure who you are to Poppy, but back the fuck off," Samuel said from my side.

Oh crap.

Jerimiah's biker brothers swarmed him, but it wasn't soon enough. Jerimiah's arm sliced out, his fist colliding with Samuel's face. Samuel stumbled back, righted and then came back with his own arm raised.

"Stop," I yelled, getting between them both with my arms up, ice bag dropped. They paused, not wanting to hurt me in the process of their fight.

"Fang, step back," a guy I didn't know said. His vest read President, so he must have been Dodge. I'd heard his name in passing.

Jerimiah didn't move, neither did Samuel.

"Dodge, a word," a detective called. Just before Fang had arrived, I'd given my statement. Only I'd lied.

"Fang, cool down," Dodge ordered, before he stepped away.

Muff moved up to Samuel and whispered something. Samuel nodded and shifted off to the end of the bar with Muff. I kind of wished they hadn't moved because then Jerimiah's attention came back to me.

His nostrils flared as he stepped back into my space. His gaze ran over my cheek, and I knew he saw the bruise already formed. His jaw clenched again, but gently, he reached up and ran the back of his fingers along my jawbone.

"Not a fan of being kept in the dark, Poppy."

I snorted. "And you wonder why I didn't tell you."

Yet another clench of his jaw. I was sure he was going to break his teeth. "Who was he?" Jerimiah demanded.

"I'm not sure." I lied, like I had to the police. It wasn't their problem. Python was a Venom member. Clubs liked to handle their own situations. Already I'd decided to go to Blackie and have him deal with Python. I didn't want to drag anyone else into my mess. Blackie was the president and he'd hate it if I brought cops into club business, so it was up to Blackie to do what he had to and make sure I never saw Python again. I knew he would. He cared for me as if I were his own daughter since Blackie and Dad were close.

Jerimiah studied me. His arm swept around my waist and he brought me flush against him. "Not liking you holding back."

"Jerimiah, I'm not—"

"Don't lie to me," he hurled harshly in my face.

Glaring, I pushed against his chest. One good thing about Jerimiah being there was that my nerves had lessened; instead, I was annoyed. "Do not talk to me like that. You can throw your Hulk attitude around, but not at me or I'll kick your arse myself."

I heard a few male chuckles around us, then, "Damn, she's a tigress."

"Shit yeah, did you see the way she laid into the motherfucker with her feet?"

Jerimiah's eyes, upon hearing that, darkened. "You had to fight him?"

"Does it matter?" I asked, pushing against him again.

"Yes," he clipped loudly.

"Fang, brother. Compound for church," Dodge called.

Jerimiah's hand tightened around my waist before he released me. "I'll be seeing you real soon, Poppy."

Rolling my eyes, I clasped my hands in front of me. "Oh, joy. I just can't wait for then."

He scowled. "Stay here until Charlie gets here."

"Yes, boss," I said, while scratching the side of my nose with my middle finger. Jerimiah's lips twitched until he glanced again at my bruise. He fisted his hands and then left with some other brothers of his.

My anger dissipated, my nerves returning, and they twisted my stomach. Charlie was going to lose his left nut over what had happened. There was no way I would be informing my dad it was Python either. Blackie would get it all, as soon as I could dodge Charlie, because I knew he wouldn't be letting me out of his sight anytime soon.

God, was I doing the right thing? Keeping people out of Venom's business? Protecting my dad? Protecting Jerimiah? I didn't know. I was out of my element, but I had to try.

Right?

CHAPTER TEN

FANG

*C*hurch was a waste of my time since it was the same old shit: up the hunting so we can protect what's ours, up the security, and discuss who was working where. After, I went to my ride, climbed on, and headed to Charlie and Poppy's. While riding, I couldn't stop from thinking what Parker had said to Dodge, that they weren't sure the man at the club was the same dick who was beating strippers. We had to find out for certain, and I reckoned Poppy had that answer.

I'd hated leaving her earlier, when I was so pissed, but seeing her standing there with a bruise on her face... it put God honest fear in my gut.

Someone could have taken her.

The motherfucker needed to be dealt with, and fast.

I parked my ride out the front and made my way to the door. One knock and it opened. Charlie stood in it with a grim look on his face. He opened the door wider, and I spotted Poppy sitting on the couch. She had her knees up to her chest and her arms curled around them. Moving in, I kept my eyes on her and sat beside her, but shifted to face her.

I heard Charlie shut the door and then caught him walking into my sight, placing himself in his armchair at the end of the couch.

"You know why I'm here, Poppy."

She said nothing. Her eyes moved down to her knees.

"Honey, you gotta tell him everything," Charlie urged.

Fuckin' knew she'd been holding out back at the club.

"Did you know the guy who tried to take you?"

Still nothing.

"He's not the same guy as the one on the news," Charlie said.

I grunted. "We thought that too, at least the police did." Scooting closer to Poppy, I nudged her foot with my knee. "Darlin', whatever it is you're worried about, don't be. You shouldn't want to protect this guy."

Her hard eyes snapped up to mine. "I'm not. I don't want to, but this is Venom business, not yours. Not

Hawks. Dad already got it out of me, but at least he's Venom."

"Poppy," Charlie barked gruffly.

"All good, Charlie," I said. "The problem is, Poppy, it is my business, and the Hawks's. It's ours more than anyone's because it happened on our property. You gotta talk to me, woman."

She puffed out a breath. "I thought… if I went to Blackie, he could handle it before it went any further."

"You can still go to Blackie, but it happened in a Hawks club, Poppy. You know we gotta do somethin' about it," I reasoned, then added, "It also happened to someone I care about, and my brother bled for it."

"I know," she replied quietly. "I know, and I'm sorry about it all." She wiped her nose then scratched above her ear. "It's my fault he was there."

"How?" I pressed.

With her eyes back down on her knees, she said, "He's a member of the Venom Motorcycle Club. When I came back to town, I was at the compound one night seeing Roda and Blackie and noticed him with his mates in the corner of the room. He'd just been patched in as a full member. We, um, chatted for a bit. He asked me out, and I went." She cleared her throat, seeming nervous about explaining it. All I wanted to do was punch something.

"She went on a couple of dates with him," Charlie added when Poppy didn't continue. My hands fisted.

Poppy noticed, so I relaxed them and stuffed them under my thighs on the couch. If she knew the anger rising about hearing her dating, she wouldn't continue.

Though she knew me, and the sad, apologetic smile she shot me told me I wasn't hiding my anger well.

"Yeah, the first date was okay, so I thought I'd give him another chance. That was when his true colours showed. He was an arse to everyone. No matter where we went. At the restaurant, the movies, the club after. He treated people like they were beneath him. Let's just say it didn't work out and when I told him there'd be no more dates... he didn't like it. Apparently, he saw me as his."

Fucking hell.

Fire erupted inside of me.

The cunt thought he had some bloody claim over my woman. At least with me my claim had somewhere to go. Poppy and I had a past. Had time with one another. She knew me like I knew her. I wasn't claiming her after a couple of goddamn dates.

The guy was mental.

"What's his name?"

"Python."

"Do you know anything you could tell me about him?"

"Muff described him, right?"

"Yeah, but I'm talking about other things. Where he hangs when he's not at the clubhouse. Outside friends, anything?"

"No." She shook her head. "He didn't talk much about himself. I'm sorry."

Shit.

"It's all right. At least we have a name."

Christ, her bottom lip wobbled. "Muff got shot because of me."

Reaching out, I placed my hand on her knee and applied pressure until I had her watery eyes. "Babe, he's fine. It was a scrape if anything. Hell, he didn't even leave the strip club when it reopened." She nodded. "He's good. Promise."

"Okay," she mumbled.

"But there's something' else we gotta talk about."

She sighed, her head going back, eyes to the ceiling. She straightened. "Let me guess, it's about me and where I work."

"Damn right."

She glanced at her father and then back. "I have to keep working, Jerimiah."

"No, Poppy," Charlie said. "It's too big of a risk."

"He got in there, yes. But now people will know who to look for, and he wouldn't be stupid enough to try again. You know we need this money coming in, Dad."

"I'll pick up extra hours—"

"No. Dad, please, the hours I work are perfect. It means we can spend time with Mum during her visiting times." Her stubborn gaze met mine. "I won't give it up."

"Poppy—"

"I won't."

Fuck. "Okay, darlin'." I nodded. Her whole body relaxed. "I'll talk to Dodge and Samuel. We'll get something set up. I don't like it, but you want it, so I'll let you have it for you and your family."

She didn't need the added pressure of not having an income to help her parents out. Not while her mum was in care.

"Thank you."

"Don't thank me, babe. Just be careful. You'll have someone at your back. If it ain't Charlie, it'll be me or another brother, but I'll be sure you know him before he takes a shift. You can't go anywhere without one of us following you."

"I promise I won't."

"Good. Now, I gotta get goin'," I said and stood. "Try and get some rest, both of you. I'll have Dallas swing by as soon as he can to check your security system. Until then, stay alert."

"We will." Charlie nodded.

"I'm sorry again," Poppy said. "I should have said something back at the club, but I did want to take care of it myself."

"Know you did. At least you've told me now. We'll get him, Poppy."

"Okay," she whispered. Leaning down, I pressed my

lips to the top of her head and then ran my fingers through her hair. Silk.

"Take care," I said, then walked to the front door. Charlie followed me out and shut the door behind himself.

"You'll keep me updated?"

"I will. You know it."

"Thanks, son." He tipped his chin to me.

"Anything for you, but especially her."

He smiled. "Know that. Be safe."

"Always try," I said, before heading to my ride. Stopping there, I grabbed my phone and hit Dodge's name in my contacts.

"Yeah, brother?"

"I have a name and know he's part of Venom."

"Fuck. Give me the name and I'll head to set up a meet with Blackie. But it'll have to be tomorrow since it's the middle of the night."

"Python."

"Got it. How'd you get this info?"

"Poppy. He was an ex of hers. She didn't want to say anything because she was gonna get Blackie to sort it out."

"This is Hawks business, was on Hawks property."

"Know that, got her to understand it."

"Good job, brother. Now, go get some bloody sleep."

"Heading to do that now."

"Talk tomorrow."

"Done," I replied, and ended the call.

I DIDN'T HEAD BACK to the compound where my bed lay. Instead, I had an urge to see my ma. Maybe it was because of what Poppy was going through with Mary, or it could have been because it'd been over a week since I'd seen her last. Whatever it was, I pulled up out front and made my way to the pitch-dark house. She'd be in bed, but at least I'd see her in the morning.

Or so I thought. Just as I reached the front door, it opened, and Ma stood in it dressed in her ratty robe. One day soon I'd buy her a new one, no matter the times she'd told me it was her favourite.

"What're you doin' outta bed, Ma?"

She smiled warmly before I folded her in my arms and kissed her temple. "Heard your bike coming, was worried why you'd visit an old lady so late."

"Nothing serious. I'm good, Ma."

She wound her arm around my waist, and after I shut and locked the front door, I placed mine around her shoulders. We walked into the kitchen. She let me go and went to the cupboard. "Coffee or a stiff drink?"

"Whisky, please."

"Right." She grabbed the bottle from the top cupboard

and a glass, then poured a two-finger width. "What's happened, Jerimiah?" she asked, placing the glass in front of me.

After a sip, I said, "Just wanted to see you."

"Not often you call in in the middle of the night. Something must have happened for you to do so."

I ran a hand over my face. Goddamn, I was knackered. "Haven't told you yet, but Poppy's back in town."

She tried, but failed, to cover her huge smile in time. "You've seen her?"

Snorting, I pushed the chair opposite me out with my foot. Ma got the hint and sat in it. "Yeah, I have. Things haven't been good for her momma. She's got dementia, sometimes refuses to eat and drink. Doesn't look good."

Ma's face fell into a concerned frown. "That's... terrible. Mary was always such a beautiful person."

When Switch left, Ma couldn't go back to Venom. For her own sake, she had to cut ties with the club. Everyone understood, but there were a couple of friendships she regretted cutting, and one was Mary. Seeing my ma, with tears filling her eyes, sliced at me.

"I should have kept in contact," she whispered.

"Mary understood. Out of any of those old ladies, Mary understood the most. Don't beat yourself up about it, Ma."

She nodded, sniffing. "I'll try."

"I know you will." And she would. She was bloody brave and strong.

"So… Poppy?"

Chuckling, I shook my head. It had always pleased her, Mary, and Charlie how close Poppy and I were. Knew they'd hoped something would come from the two of us more than friendship. Guessed it was time to mention to Mum her wish would be true soon enough.

"It's gonna be hard, but yeah, Ma. Poppy'll be mine." She clapped, stood, and I warned, "Do not do it, woman."

Too late. She was already doing her own happy jig.

CHAPTER ELEVEN

POPPY

*D*ad and I left the house early to visit Mum. I'd chosen the dress she'd loved most on me. It was a rock-a-billy blue dress that Mum had picked out when we'd gone shopping one day. She'd gushed over it so much, I'd just had to have it because she'd loved it on me, after she'd forced me to try it on. I wore it in the hope she was having a good day and remembered me.

It was terrible. I *felt* terrible, because as I approached her door, I couldn't help the burning in my chest or stomach, fearing she wouldn't know me.

Dad gripped my hand before releasing it and stepping

up to open the door first, while I sucked in a much-needed deep breath and braced myself.

"My moon," I heard from my mum, and I almost choked on a sob. Another intake of a deep breath helped me centre myself. She'd recognised Dad.

"My sky," Dad replied, his voice thick with emotion.

When Dad shifted towards her and I was in view, her smile brightened even more. "My star," she whispered. Tears swam in her eyes like I knew mine were too. She'd always, *always* called Dad her moon, me her star, and Alvin had been her sun, while she was the sky. She'd said our family filled the earth with everything necessary.

"Hey, Mum," I mumbled.

Dad leaned down to her, cupping her cheek and when she dragged her gaze from me to him, he said, "Love you more than breathing."

She sniffed. "Love you more than seeing."

God. *God.* I had to thin my lips and blink rapidly to stop from bursting into tears. Their love. I wanted to have their type of love for my own one day. I'd never seen a couple who were married after forty years and still so in love with one another.

"Come here, my sweet girl," Mum called. Dad sat at her far side, curling his arm around her shoulders and tucking her close. I picked her other side, where I could lie next to her. I slid my arm around her waist while hers cradled around my shoulders, and I leaned into her.

I clenched my jaw. It hurt. Hurt so much. She'd lost more weight.

However, having these moments, when she was herself, were moments I would cherish, even if they were far and few.

She cleared her throat. "The nurse told me why I'm in here, and I got your letter, my sky. I'm sorry."

Dad made a noise in the back of his throat. "Mary—"

"No. Please, don't. The heartache I saw on you both when you arrived… it crushed my chest, and I need you both to know how sorry I am you have to go through this with me."

Closing my eyes tightly, I bit down on my bottom lip. On the rare moments when Mum was Mum, she went through these words each and every time. We'd tried to stop her speaking about it, feeling regret, but it was best to let her have her say, and then we could go about remembering the good times. Dad had written her a letter a while ago and asked the nurse to tell everyone who entered Mum's room if she was having a good day or moment, to pass on the letter so she knew everything that had happened. One thing Dad never mentioned was where Alvin truly was. If she asked, we mentioned he was overseas working. We didn't want her to stress about him.

She sniffed and laid a hand on Dad's leg. The other

stroked my hair. Then she asked, "Now, tell me some happy things going on."

"Poppy and Jerimiah are back talking. Things are looking good for them, my moon."

"Dad!" I scolded. Mum laughed.

"What? She loved that boy for you."

Mum smiled. "I did. Well, I still do if you think you could be happy with him."

Catching her eyes, I said with a blush coating my cheeks, "Yes. I think I can."

She studied my face, her smile widening. "Yes, I believe you will." She kissed my forehead then brought Dad's hand up and kissed his wrist. "I want you all happy."

"We are, my moon."

"I'm so very glad."

"Love you, Mum."

"I know." She nodded. "And I love you. I love all my family."

"But especially me," Dad piped up, causing Mum to laugh.

PAST

POPPY

Dad had asked me to go to the compound, but I chose not to. Instead, I was home with Mum, and we were having a girl day. Mum always said it was good to have girl days and spoil ourselves. What I loved about it was just spending time with Mum talking, okay, gossiping, and eating what we wanted without Alvin or Dad stealing it. We also loved to watch movies and do our nails.

"Poppy?" she called. She sat on the couch while I was on the floor beside her legs, with one foot up on my thigh while I painted her toenails a bright red.

"Yeah," I mumbled, concentrating on what I was doing.

"My star," she said.

I laughed. "Yes, Mum?"

"Honey, I want your eyes for a moment." Her tone was serious, the humour of a few moments ago gone. We'd been laughing about Manda and how she put a paper bag of dog poop on the front step of Jeff's house. Jeff being her ex who cheated on her. She'd set the bag on fire, rang the bell, then ran for it. She'd filmed the whole thing: how Jeff came out, started stamping on the bag and got shit all over himself. It'd been the best scene ever.

Twisting on the lid to the nail polish, I sat it down on the carpet and turned to face Mum. She leaned forward, a smile on her lips, so whatever she had to say couldn't have been that serious.

"Your dad and I know about Jerimiah sneaking into your room at night."

Oh, shit.

My body froze, my heart racing while I waited for the lecture to come. Waited for her to tell me Jerimiah wouldn't be allowed to do it again, and waited for her to tell me I had to spend less time with him.

It didn't come.

Instead, her smile widened.

"It's okay," she said.

"Say what now?" I blurted, my brows shooting up in shock.

She giggled. "There isn't a boy who we'd trust you with completely. Except Jerimiah."

"For real?" I asked, awe in my voice.

"Yes. He's proven himself to us on many times. Your dad adores him for you. I do too. So much. We respect him."

I grinned. "He is pretty awesome."

"He is." She paused. "Do you have strong feelings for him, more than just a friend?"

I glanced away, but Mum caught my chin with her

fingers and dragged my gaze back to hers. She smiled softly. "You do."

"Yes."

"We just worry because you're both so young."

"I'm sixteen. I know what love is."

She shook her head. "I'm not saying you don't. The bond you and Fang have is something amazing. It reminds me of your Dad and me. A love that'll last a life-time. All we want is for you to not rush things."

"I won't. I promise, but… do you really think he loves me back?"

"Yes, my star. I really do, but I think he's waiting for the right time."

I felt giddy hearing someone else say Jerimiah loved me. I'd always hoped, prayed. It wasn't the same coming from Manda, but my mum knew a lot. She was wise, so if she'd said it, it must be true.

It was later that night, with courage tucked into socks, I went in search for Jerimiah. I heard he was at a party, so I caught a taxi to the house. Only, when I found him, I wished I hadn't.

Not wanting to go through the front door of the party, I snuck around the side and paused at the gate, looking over. It was then I saw him.

He was sitting on a lawn chair with some stupid bitch I didn't know on his lap. They were that close I heard everything they'd said.

"You gonna come back to my room?" Jerimiah slurred.

The girl giggled. "Maybe. But only if you can tell me what's up with you and that red-haired girl."

"Poppy?"

"Yeah. She your girl?"

He snorted. "Shit no."

"Why do you hang with her all the time then?"

"Her dad and mine are in the same club. She follows me around all the damn time, can't get rid of her. It's a nuisance really. She doesn't mean anything to me... but you, you could."

Bile rose. I clutched my stomach. Pain from his words cut me deeply over and over.

I wasn't anything to him.

I meant nothing.

I was a nuisance.

God. It crippled me.

"Yeah?" she giggled.

"Oh, yeah." He kissed her.

Jerimiah kissed her.

And I ran.

And I kept running until I found myself at the Venom compound.

"Nothing," I whispered harshly to myself. "I was nothing to him." Sneaking into the kitchen, I went in search of something to drown my sorrows in. To make myself get lost so I couldn't remember. I wanted to forget his words.

In the walk-in refrigerator, I grabbed the first bottle I saw, unscrewed it and took a big gulp. But then I heard footsteps, and then the door behind me opening wider.

Slowly, I turned, and dread filled me.

Switch. Jerimiah's dad was standing there with a look in his eyes.

A look that scared me to my bones.

WITH TEARS STREAKING down my face, I quickly opened the front door and closed it, locking it. Mum jumped from the couch. "Poppy?"

I shook my head over and over.

Running to my room, I went in and paused. What did I do?

I had to get out of here.

"Poppy, what is it? What happened?" Mum asked, fear in her voice as she bolted into my room after me.

Turning, I grabbed her hand. "Mum, you have to help me. Please, please, help me."

"What happened?"

"They'll kill him. They'll kill him, and we'll lose them forever."

Bile rose once again but because I was on the verge of panic. My mind was jumbled. I just wanted to shower, to hide, to scream.

"Who will kill who? Please, my star, talk to me."

"I have to go away," I said, stalking to my closet and grabbing my suitcase. I pulled it down and threw it on my bed. An idea popped in, a ray of hope through the desperation swirling inside. "Not long ago Aunt Maris said I could stay with her for a while, right? I have to go there." Opening a drawer, I grabbed random clothes and threw them in the bag.

Mum took hold of my arm, dragged me around to face her, and placed her hands firmly on my shoulders. "Honey, you're scaring me. Tell me what's going on."

My tears welled, I sniffed. "Jerimiah... I heard him say some mean things about me to a girl."

"He probably wasn't thinking. He's eighteen, honey, and fighting with himself over loving a younger girl."

I shook my head. "It doesn't matter. M-maybe I'll get through the hurt one day, but right now, it doesn't matter."

"Why?"

Glancing to the floor, I sucked in a breath and blew it out. I then looked up to meet Mum's concerned eyes. "I went to the compound to... I wanted a drink. Switch was there. H-he touched me, Mum." She gasped. "Blackie helped me... got me away from him. But... Mum, if Jerimiah and Dad find out, they'll kill him and we'll lose them. I have to go."

"No." Her eyes shone with anger. It was so bright I had to look away. "We have to tell them—"

"No!" I cried. "Please, I can't do that to them. They'll go to jail. I won't have that on me. I won't. Blackie said it's not the right time, but he'll pay for it. Switch will pay, just not yet."

Her eyes softened. "My star, they have a right—"

"And I have a right to protect them both. It's what *I* want, Mum. Please help me help them."

She frantically searched my face. Never had I begged my parents for anything, but with the need to protect two people I loved, I didn't even hesitate, even when my insides were still dying from Jerimiah's words. Still, there was no way I wouldn't protect him. We'd been friends for so long, been through so much.

"All right," Mum whispered. "I'll call your aunt and organise it."

My whole body sagged in relief. "Thank you."

"You're a beautiful soul, my star. So strong, and wise. I love you."

"I love you, Mum."

She kissed my forehead. "Pack. I'll call, and we'll leave early in the morning."

"But Dad."

"We have to tell him something, else he won't let you go. Let me think on it. He'll need to see you before you go."

"Okay." I nodded.

An hour later I was ready for my morning trip. I heard Dad arrive home and Mum calling for his attention. I went to my door and opened it a little.

"My moon, I have to talk to you about something."

"What's wrong?"

"Come sit for a moment."

"Darlin', you're worrying me."

"Poppy and Jerimiah had a fight. She's very upset."

He snorted. "She'll get over it or he will."

"This is different. She wants to go stay with my sister for a while, and I think it's the best choice. They're so young, Charlie. Made for each other, but too young. I think time apart will be good for them."

"I don't like it, Mary. Don't like our girl away from us."

"I know, and it'll be hard, but for their future, we could at least give it a try for a while."

"Shit. What did Jerimiah do so bad?"

"I can't say. I promised Poppy I wouldn't."

"Just tell me if I need to put some hurt on him?"

Mum laughed. "No. Things will work out in the end."

"All right, my sky. I trust you to know what you're doing."

The love I had for Mum at that moment was huge.

Then again, it had always been big. But her having my back meant so much to me, and together, we protected Dad and Jerimiah.

CHAPTER TWELVE

PRESENT

POPPY

*W*e stayed with Mum for over two hours, and when she started to get tired, we decided to leave. Not that we wanted to. But towards the end, she started to get confused about things, and in our own selfish way, we wanted to go so we had a good visit with Mum remembering us.

Guilt gnawed at the both of us for feeling that way; we'd spoken openly about it many times. Still, I would take the guilt times one hundred since we got to actually spend time with Mum and have her remember who we were.

Just as we pulled into the drive, Dad's phone rang. He shut off the car, and answered it, "Yo?" He went silent, and then very still while he listened to whoever was on the other end. His brows dipped, and his hand on the steering wheel tightened.

Something was wrong.

"Got it. Yep. Right," he answered, and then hung up.

"What happened?" I asked straight away.

"Let's get inside."

"Dad, what happened? Is it Jerimiah?"

"No, honey. Let's get inside and we'll talk."

"Dad!"

"Fuck. Stubborn as me you are." He sighed. "Honey, none of it's your fault. Fang wanted me to confirm with you that you need to understand that."

I froze.

"Honey?"

"What happened?" I asked coldly.

"There was a drive-by at the Hawks garage. They think it was Python, but they're not sure yet."

"Who?"

"Who what?"

"Who was hurt?" *Or dead?* But I couldn't bring myself to ask that. Already I felt the need to vomit just knowing

Python had targeted Hawks in a goddamn drive-by because of me.

"A brother of theirs was taken to hospital. It doesn't look good. Another was shot in the shoulder."

I closed my eyes, tipped my head back and banged it into the headrest. "All because of me. All because of me."

"Poppy, honey," Dad tried.

"No." I stopped banging enough to shake my head and open my door. Leaping from the car, I ran to the house and managed to unlock it with my own set of keys even before Dad got close. I didn't want his comfort. I didn't deserve it. I'd got blood on my hands because Python picked me to claim, picked me to haunt and make my life hell. In turn, I got people shot, and one was near death.

It was my fault.

Running for my room as Dad shouted my name, I got inside and slammed the door closed. After locking it, I grunted as I pushed my drawers in front of the door.

It was a childish move. To run and hide. But I had to be alone. I had to breathe, to think by myself.

Leaning my back against the drawers, I rubbed at my chest. Gripping my hair, I tried to calm myself down…. I couldn't. Because of me, people bled.

People could die because of me.

"Poppy?" I heard muffled outside of my room.

"Please, please, please, just leave me alone."

I needed to be alone. To breathe. To think *and* feel.

"Honey," he pressed. "It's not your—"

"No. Stop! It is. It is."

How could anyone not see it? It was my fault. And how could they possibly forgive me?

FANG

In yet another meeting, we learned Blackie had confirmed it was Python's vehicle used for the drive-by. Blackie had cut Python from the Venom Motorcycle Club, not wanting war with Hawks, and also, the mother-fucker was a drug dealer looking to branch out into our territory.

He'd already been on our hit list, but the drive-by was the last straw.

Dodge called my name, breaking me from my thoughts. Moving my eyes from the table, I turned slightly to Dodge. "What?" I barked.

"You able to hold it together?"

The fucker scared and touched Poppy. He still wanted her and hadn't liked Hawks being around her. He shot not one, but three brothers, leaving one in a bad way. Was I gonna be able to hold it together? No. But I'd fuckin' try so I didn't lose out on getting my chance with the cunt. "Yes," I clipped my lie.

"Brother, know she's been in your past—"

"She'll be my future soon," I declared.

"Until then, we know she's somethin' to you, and this Python guy wants her, but you gotta keep a clear head. Not only for you, but for her too."

"I will," I stated darkly. I had to keep it together until I got my hands on him.

"Isn't her dad a Venom?" someone called out.

My chair slammed into the floor as I stood. "So fuckin' what? I used to be one as well, and I still got some mates left in that club. You got a problem with it? Not gonna have my back now?"

No one said anything.

"We got your back, brother," Vicious, of all people, called. "Need all the info we have on Python. Did you used to hang with him in the day?"

Sucking in a deep breath, I ran a hand over my head, and then shook it. Drawing back in some rage, I said, "No, he's a new recruit. Got in just after I left. Poppy didn't actually date him. They went on a couple of dates, but she didn't like what she saw, so she refused to go out with him again. He didn't like that. Claimed her without telling her, so he thinks he owns her."

"Does she know where he hangs when not at Venom's compound?" Billy asked.

"No. *Two dates*, that's all she had with him, and he didn't give her much information on himself." Two goddamn motherfuckin' dates with a cunt. It should have been me. I should have been in her life so that hadn't happened.

"So we got nothin' to go on to find the fucker?" Dallas asked.

"If he's that obsessed with her, he'll come lookin' again," Muff said.

Rage flared once again. "She'll not be bait," I roared.

"Fuck me, calm the hell down, brother. No one said anything about bait. It's an obvious fact he's got it bad for her. We'll keep her protected," Dodge stated.

"What's the plan then?" Griz put in.

"We go to the street, find out who's been buyin' off Python, and see what they know of the guy," Handle suggested.

Dodge nodded. "Good. We still got businesses to run so we'll be rotating everything around between all of us. I'll get Low and Josie on it, and you'll get a text or email with the roster. I'm headin' out with Killer, Stoke, Gamer, and Griz. We're goin' back to Venom's to talk to their new recruits, see if any of them came in with Python. Got the feelin' from Blackie the guy isn't smart enough to work alone. Someone's gotta know somethin'." His eyes came to me. "Fang and Vicious, you're both on Poppy. Watch her like a hawk, brothers." Finally. It was about damn time I got outta there to head to the place I wanted to be. Vicious and I got up at the same time and walked out.

Out the front, Vicious grabbed my arm before I climbed on my ride. "You got her tonight. I'll come by in the morning and change shifts."

Still blew my mind Vicious, even after the past we'd had, was willing to have my back, and help me out with my woman.

"I'll talk with Charlie. See when he'll be around or not, and we'll work around him."

"Got it." Then the fucker gave me a pat on the shoulder. "Good luck taming that one."

Glaring, I watched him walk away. Shit, I was probably gonna need all the help I could get, but I knew Poppy, so I knew she'd be blaming herself for it all. I had to get there, reassure her, and confirm she understood we'd always protect her. Hawks would because I was their brother and she was gonna be my woman.

Charlie was already sitting on the front porch when I pulled up. He stood as I approached. "She won't talk to me, won't listen. Condemning herself about all that motherfucker's actions. All because he took notice of her. She... fuck, Fang. She's not good. Soon as we got home from visiting Mary, she locked herself away, shoved shit against it so I can't break it down."

"Give me some time with her," I said, and then started around the house.

"Where you goin'?" Charlie called.

"Gettin' into her." Jogging down the side of the house, I stopped at her window. It was all the way down, and I could see the lock in place. Shit, my woman had shifted her dresser over to the door. She didn't want company. Instead, she wanted to wallow without anyone helping her.

Too bad.

Shifting, I lifted my leather-clad arm and smashed the glass to her window with my elbow.

Her scream cut short when she noticed it was me. "What the hell, Jerimiah?"

Pulling myself through the window, after knocking the rest of the glass out, I said, "You won't talk to your dad. Barred the door, so it was my only option."

She moved to the side of the bed, her feet coming to the floor. "You didn't think to knock on the bloody window first?"

"Would you have opened it for me?" I questioned, my brows rising.

She opened her mouth, then snapped it shut. Poppy glared, harrumphed, and then shifted on the bed so she lay with her back to me.

"Exactly what I thought. Now you've got no way of not listening to me." Kicking off my boots, I slipped off my jacket, then club vest, which I placed at the end of the bed. Then, I deposited my gun on the bedside table before I climbed on the bed and moved to match the front of me to her back.

Only before I could say anything, her breath hitched as she said, "I'm sorry. I'm so sorry this is happening to you, your brothers, and all because of me."

"It's not your fault, darlin'."

"H-how can you say that when it was me who went out with him, and me who made him notice the Hawks? It was me he was getting back at by shooting up your place."

Sliding my arm around her waist, I grabbed her hand and held it with mine. "Jesus, Poppy. He's not right in the head, and that ain't your fuckin' fault. You didn't ask him to do any of that. It's ain't on you, baby."

"It's easy for you to say, Jerimiah, but not easy for me to think otherwise."

"None of my brothers blame you. None."

"Is… your brother who was critical…?"

"He pulled through the op. He's gonna be okay, and I can tell you now, not even Elvis will blame you for any of this."

She shrugged. Letting go of her hand, I flicked back her hair and leaned my mouth close to her ear. "Not sure how I can get you to believe, baby, but know this, if I blamed you for any of it, I wouldn't be here. I wouldn't hold you like I am."

"I know," she whispered. "I think," she added, her tone

serious. When I growled in the back of my throat, she let out a laugh.

"Need some sleep, darlin', and I'm doin' it right here."

She snorted. "Well, since you broke my window, I guess I don't have a choice on the matter."

"No, you don't." I grinned. It wasn't until she'd fallen asleep that I flew off a text to Muff about Poppy's window needing to be fixed first thing in the morning. As soon as he replied with laughing emojis—the dick—he said he'd get right onto it. Then I curled myself around my woman and slept like I hadn't in years. Peacefully.

CHAPTER THIRTEEN

FANG

*I*t'd been a goddamn hectic week since the shooting. I'd spent it working, hunting along with Lan and Parker, who seemed they were on the case too, visiting a recovering Elvis, and in between all that, kept an eye on Poppy. That was when Charlie or Vicious wasn't following her around or sitting out the front watching the house when she was inside alone. I'd given her time away from me in person. Time to think. She needed to understand we'd never hold a grudge against her for what had happened. She needed to come to terms with it on her own, without me.

But that time ended tonight.

Shit, at least I gave her a week.

I'd just come from the hospital after chatting with Elvis and headed to Pick and Billy's pub. I needed a drink, then some goddamn sleep. Though, I wasn't sure I'd be getting any since I'd called Charlie earlier and suggested Poppy needed a break from the house and everything else she did. I mentioned the pub, and to also get Manda, who'd just moved back to town for a high-paying job, and no doubt to keep a better eye on her friend, on board with the idea. Knew Manda wouldn't let Poppy shy away from walking into a Hawks business. She'd been a nut back in the day, and still was from what Charlie said.

Also, if Poppy came, it meant she was on her way to believing none of this bullshit was her fault. At least that was what I hoped it meant.

Making my way to the bar, I greeted the brothers around with chin lifts or nods. Pick was behind the bar serving. "How was Elvis?" he asked.

"Doin' okay." I nodded.

"Good. Beer, brother?" he asked.

"Yeah." I nodded and then felt heat at my back. Turning, I found Manda and Poppy standing there. Manda was looking up at me and grinning like a fool, while Poppy glanced around the place apprehensively. Shit, she was still worried my brothers and I were pissed at her for the cunt gunning after Hawks. It didn't seem to matter how many times I told her we weren't. I could see she still felt guilty. Maybe the night would ease her mind if she met a few more of the brothers.

"Hiya, Jerimiah," Manda said.

"Fang, Manda."

"Right, Fang." She flicked a look at Poppy, and then back. "But Poppy calls you Jerimiah."

"Only her," I stated, and finally Poppy's wide-eyed gaze hit mine. I winced at the sight of her bruise; it'd gone down a bit, but it was still noticeable. My temper rose, my hands twitching, wanting to wrap them around a certain someone.

I took a deep breath and eyed my woman. She looked amazing, no matter the bruising, and fuck, it'd been a while since I'd laid eyes on her. Jesus, I had to have a conversation with my cock to stop from growing hard in a goddamn biker bar. Her clothes were simple, jeans and a tee, yet they fitted her perfectly. Her long red hair was braided down her back, and she had on light make-up, trying to cover her discolouring. I wanted to reach out and take her in my arms, crush my mouth to hers, and claim her right in front of everyone.

Her eyes widened even more, and I wondered if she knew where my thoughts had gone.

"Got ya," Manda said, and I'd fuckin' forgot what we were even talking about.

"Have a seat," I suggested. Taking my beer Pick placed

down, I stepped back from the bar so they could grab the two free seats. Manda sat quickly, leaning over the bar a bit to order for her and Poppy. I could have laughed at the way she eyed Pick and told her she didn't stand a chance, but I left it. Hell, Pick had his fair share of women trying to get his attention. Only no one stood a chance. He was happy with Josie and Billy.

Poppy slid past me, and I had to touch her in some way, so I ran my fingers down her back, then smirked when she stumbled forward. Her hands went to the bar to right herself. I took her waist to help steady her, guiding her onto the seat.

"I've got it," she said with a glare over her shoulder. Winking, I stifled my chuckle with a sip of my beer. Goddamn, it was good to have her around me. My gut had been eating at itself in torment from everything that had happened recently, but most of all, for not having Poppy close to my side as my woman. Life was too bloody short. The shooting was proof of that. Anything could happen, and I was tired of living with regret from losing her.

"Manda, how's it goin' being back in Caroline Springs?" I asked.

She shrugged. "It's only been a few days, but I like it so far. Get to keep a better eye on my girl here." She winked at Poppy, and then when she looked back my way, her eyes moved over my shoulder and widened. "And now I'm liking it even more."

"Hey, brother. Who's the new bird?" Muff stepped up to my side and ran his gaze over Manda. A smirk touched his lips. He liked what he saw. Then his gaze landed on Poppy, "Tigress," he teased.

"Tigress?" Manda asked.

"Ah…" was all Poppy said.

"I was there when that dickhead tried to take her for a chat. Got the scar to prove it." He grinned, lifting up his tee on his arm. Dropping it back down, he winked at Manda. "Name's Muff."

Manda started giggling.

"And don't let him start some story about his name." The women turned to Pick as he lay their drinks down. Muff grumbled under his breath about having cockhead brothers.

"So what does it mean?" Manda asked.

"That I love a certain area of a woman's body," Muff announced quickly. I snorted. That wasn't it at all. Ever since Muff had heard Dive's story about his name—how Dive liked to dive into pussy—Muff was in awe that it worked for all the women, so he changed the meaning behind his road name. I wasn't sure if it worked for him, but the dude would try anything.

Pick snorted, leaning his hip into the bar. Jason, who

was also serving laughed outright, while I caught Poppy's eyes and rolled mine.

"His name's short for Muffler," I explained. Apparently, when Muff was a young boy in the club, he'd got caught with his dick in the end of a muffler, so hence the name Muff. I wasn't sure if that story was true, but hell, I wouldn't put it past Muff. He seemed to have new pussy every goddamn night. Some said he was a nymphomaniac, or the male version a satyriasis.

And that was shit you just didn't need to know about a brother.

"Pick, Josie comin' in tonight?" I asked.

"Nah, brother. She's out with Billy." He grinned. "They're on a hot date. Then they're goin' in to see Elvis," he added, before disappearing down the other end of the bar when someone called.

"Who's Josie?" Manda asked, and I didn't miss the brief glance between friends. She was asking for Poppy.

Smiling, I said, "Josie's Pick's woman." I left it at that and took a swig of beer. Muff started chuckling at my side at the confused looks both women displayed.

"But… Pick just said she was on a hot date with some Billy guy."

I nodded. "Yep. Billy the Kid, another brother."

Poppy flicked her gaze between Muff and me, finally settling on me. "So she's dating the both of them?"

"Yeah." I winked.

Manda gasped. "And they're okay with that? With sharing?"

Muff snorted. "Pretty much anything goes in our club, and we wouldn't want it any other way."

"Damn right," I agreed. If we were like the Venom MC, my old club, it's sad to say even with Blackie as prez, they wouldn't allow gay guys in. Hawks was different. With Beast and Knife coming out, they could be who they wanted to be without judgement from their brothers. And if anyone was game enough to judge, like Alvin had, then they weren't worth knowing. Times had goddamn changed, and the Hawks MC were up with those changes. Didn't mean we weren't badarse motherfuckers. We were when we had to be. We all had blood on our hands, from one time or another, and soon I'd have more. We did it to protect. To keep safe what we regarded the most.

Family.

It was another main reason I got out of Venom and into Hawks. I respected their values. Hawks was a clean club. They fought for their family and friends. Protected those who couldn't, and if shit came our way, like it had, we made sure to leave a message with whoever tried, that we weren't a club to be fucked over.

When I changed clubs, my mum was over the bloody moon happy. Jesus, I never thought I'd see her with tears flowing while she did some ecstatic jig in the kitchen.

She'd heard of Hawks, always wanted them for me, but would never have pushed me into anything. The day Switch left was the day my mum changed, and it was for the better. Hawks loved her. She'd started to, and did it often, visit the compound with homecooked meals, winning all the brothers' hearts. Then she met Jenny, Blue's mother, and Memphis's woman, they became fast friends and soon my mother was out clothes shopping, or going to the spa, movies, lunches, and other shit women did. She never used to do that back in the day because Switch hated her being independent, hated her having friends. The ones she did, like Mary, were secret ones. My ma's confidence gained each day, and I couldn't be prouder.

If Switch ever came back, I'd make sure she never saw his face. I'd have him buried so deep no one would ever find him.

A bump on my side had me looking down. "You okay?" Poppy leaned up to whisper. Her top teeth came over her bottom lip and bit down.

Easing her mind, I nodded. "Yeah, sorry, just thinkin' about Ma." I noticed Muff was talking to Manda, who seemed to be soaking up his attention. Great, I'd have to warn him off, and if he didn't listen, kick his arse.

Poppy smiled. It was good to see after everything. "How is she?"

I ran my gaze over her face. I would give anything to

just lean in and touch my mouth to hers, but I didn't. "Fantastic." Hell, she was more than fantastic; she was over the goddamn moon thrilled Poppy was back in town and in my life. She always adored Poppy. Knew something special would happen between us. Ma was nearly as upset as I was when Poppy disappeared. I became angry at the world. Didn't help I still had Switch in my life. He didn't get gone until I was in college. Then I'd met Nary, met the Hawks, and I knew life was made to be more.

However, when Poppy was around, I knew life was worth living.

"Yeah?" she asked.

"Yeah. She's living it good, always out with her friends. She's got a part-time job doing some beauty course." I chuckled. "She tried to explain *in detail* all about it, but I must have zoned out and she gave up."

She started laughing, which was music to my ears. "She always knew when you zoned. Though, it was pretty easy to tell."

Snorting, I agreed. "I really should have practiced hiding it better." Grinning, I added, "You should come see her one day. She thought the world of you."

She stiffened. I was close enough to her side to feel her whole body grow ridged. "Um, sure." She nodded. "One day."

Yeah, one day. First I had to make sure she'd be safe.

CHAPTER FOURTEEN

POPPY

*I*t felt as though my heart was expanding in my chest for Jerimiah. Despite everything that had happened because of me, he was real. Being real. About us.

I knew he'd been real on the phone about it all a while ago, but I'd denied it to keep my sanity.

I loved him in high school, but did I love him now?

Butterflies took flight in my belly, and my hands shook with the realisation.

Yes. I loved him. How could I not? He'd stayed in my heart, locked away tight since the day I met him. He was my Jerimiah.

What I couldn't understand fully was how could he care for me when I'd dropped trouble right into his and his family's life? Still, he did. Jerimiah cared for me.

Hell, we hadn't even kissed, yet I loved him again.

Jerimiah could totally suck at kissing. He could be a guy who slobbered all over a woman's face. He could also hold a woman wrong, like... their head at an odd angle while he tortured their mouths with his lips and tongue.

His sexy kissable lips.

I quickly took a sip of the wine that Manda had ordered to stop myself daydreaming about having those lips on me. How he'd trail sweet little kisses all over my body while I lay back on the bed, begging for more.... Fuck. Looking at lips led me straight into bedroom thoughts. That wasn't good.

"Watcha thinkin', darlin'?" My body jolted when his warm breath brushed the back of my neck, just behind my ear. I sank my teeth into my bottom lip to stop the moan. "Baby, you're burning up. I'd love to know what's on your mind that has you so hot and bothered."

Jesus. I knew my face, and probably neck, were matching my hair, but being around the stupid, sexy man wasn't good for me.

Wait, why was I holding back again?

Oh, that was right. Python. Somehow, I had to get rid of him and out of my life for good, and then I could move on. I need to make sure my troubles didn't follow me and cause more damage than they already had.

Then there was also what I needed to share about Switch.

But Python was my main problem. It could have been Jerimiah in intensive care.

I was already struggling to forgive myself for the attack on Elvis, but if it had been Jerimiah... I wouldn't be able to live with it.

I had to make sure everything was sorted before I moved forward with Jerimiah. If not, I would lose myself as soon as he touched me, well, in a way that wasn't teasing. Like he was right then, with his hand circling my lower back.

"Yo," I heard, so I turned away from Jerimiah's warm breath fanning my neck, sending shivers through my body, to try and look over Jerimiah's shoulder. Only he didn't move an inch. He just sighed long and loud.

He straightened and shifted. Then I saw Nary standing there. My stomach twisted. Beside her was a good-looking guy who had his arm around her shoulders. My eyes widened a fraction. He must be the guy she'd left Jerimiah for. Yes, he was good-looking, in a rough type of biker way, but he had nothing on Jerimiah.

"Hi, I'm Nary, and this is Saxon or as his brothers call him, Vicious," she said, looking right at me with a nice smile on her lips. She was pretty... no, gorgeous, even with the scar on the side of her face. Her man leaned into her and kissed her scar. Her smile widened as she looked up at him with adoration in her eyes.

They were totally in love with one another.

I shot a glance at Jerimiah to see if it was bothering him, seeing them together, but it wasn't. In fact, he was fighting his own smile as he watched them.

When Nary's eyes came back to me, I thrust my hand out, and said, "Hi, I'm Poppy. Nice to meet you both." I'd seen Vicious sitting out the front of my place, protecting me when Charlie or Jerimiah couldn't. I just didn't know who he was to Nary.

She took my hand, then squeezed once. Only it wasn't in a bitchy way. That told me she didn't mind me being around Jerimiah. If anything, it was friendly. "It's great to finally meet you," she said.

My head jerked back in shock. Finally meet me? Just what had she heard? Everything? Bringing trouble to the club?

She laughed. "Don't worry, I don't know much. All Saxon told me was that a person from Fang's life was back in it, and that you seemed to have gotten his knickers in a twist." Her eyes widened. "But in a good way," she quickly added, giggling.

Oh, well, that was a relief. I guess. At least I found myself smiling.

Jerimiah groaned, palmed his forehead, and reached

out to smack the back of Vicious's head, who in return gave him a dirty look.

"And about that guy not leaving you alone," she mentioned.

"I'm sorry," I blurted. Jerimiah got closer, and his hand slid to the back of my neck.

Her brows shot up. "Sorry about what?"

"Everything that's happened since… just everything." I dipped my chin.

"Poppy," Nary called quietly. I lifted my face. "One day I'll tell you my full story. For now, you need to know it's not your fault. None of it's your fault. Don't worry about Hawks. They're strong. I promise you they are, and they wouldn't fight if they didn't believe in what they're fighting for."

Moving my gaze from Nary to her man, to Jerimiah, I noticed they all agreed with Nary. Vicious with his chin lift, and Jerimiah with his warm smile. But didn't they understand I wasn't Hawks?

"But… I'm not a member of—"

"Don't say it," Jerimiah clipped with another squeeze to my neck. "You're a part of my life, and I'm Hawks."

Nary giggled. "You'll learn once a brother makes up his mind, there's no going back."

Rolling my eyes, I smiled. "Are they always so annoying?"

She laughed outright. "Yes."

"Angel, how about you leave the girl talk when your man and his brothers aren't around? We gotta get goin' anyway."

"Right." Nary nodded. "Listen, I'm sure the Hawks women would love to meet you—"

"Why?" I asked, my voice unnaturally high. It gained Manda's attention away from Muff.

Nary grinned, and ignoring my question, she said, "We do have to go, but I'll get your number off Jerimiah and we'll organise a get-together."

Why was I suddenly scared?

Usually women and I didn't mix. Manda was my one and only girlfriend because other women were bitches. Still, I had a feeling Nary and her friends would be different. At least I hoped.

"Can Manda come along?" She was like my security blanket who could talk to anyone. So if I messed up in any way, I knew Manda would help dissolve any issues.

Jerimiah's hand slid from my neck to my shoulder, and he leaned in to press his lips to my temple. My stomach dipped as if it was on a roller coaster. He liked my agreeing, and I liked that it had made him happy.

"Sure. We'd love that." She smiled at Manda. "I'm Nary."

I saw it then, the smile Nary produced, a sweet, kind

one. One without a trace of fake in it at all, and it won Manda over instantly. "Manda, Poppy's best friend, and we'd love to get together. Can you teach me to be a badarse biker babe?" she asked.

Nary laughed. "I could try." She looked back to me. "Talk soon."

Vicious gave us all another chin lift in farewell, while Jerimiah who glared at him, and Muff smiled, returning his gesture. Pure biker language.

"I have to go to the ladies' room," Manda announced, then stood and grabbed my wrist. "She's coming with me."

Jerimiah smirked, then took a pull from his beer.

"Do women have a secret meeting place in there? Youse always go in pairs," Muff commented. "Wait, do you watch each other piss? Is this why?"

Snorting, I shook my head. "It's so we can talk about guys without you two overhearing."

His head jerked back. "Seriously? Why don't you tell us to get lost for a while and then do it here?"

Manda scoffed. "Ah, there are bikers everywhere. I'm sure they'd tell you what was said."

His eyes narrowed before he grinned. "Is this because you like me? I'm single, babe. No need to run off and ask your girl there. Not that she'd know. She's new to the club."

"I'm not in the club," I said without thinking; actually, it was automatic.

"You are," Jerimiah stated, his tone low and growly.

"Oh my." Manda sighed, and from the far-off dazed look in her eyes, she was probably picturing Jerimiah growling over her in bed.

"Hey," I snapped, and clicked my fingers in front of her face. She shook her head and met my gaze. "Not yours."

Shit damn. I stiffened when I heard a throaty chuckle.

"Then whose am I, Poppy?" Jerimiah purred. At least I'd call it a purr because it was sultry and deep.

Ignoring him, I squeaked out, "Bathroom." Then *I* led Manda away with me.

Once inside, I glanced under the doors of the cubicles to make sure no one was in there. After all, I was in a Hawks pub. Any of their babes could be in the room and listening. When I saw no feet, I spun to Manda and ran a hand over my face, sighing. "What am I doing?"

"Getting what you want." Manda smiled.

"Remind me again. What do I want?"

"Fang in your arms, bed, and body. His delicious dark eyes haven't strayed from you since we arrived. God, I'm becoming horny from just watching him."

"Manda!"

Her hands went up in front of her. "What? It's not like

I'd do anything." She stepped up to me, placing her hands on my shoulders. Then she shook the heck out of me.

"What are you doing?" I slapped at her arms.

"Shaking some sense into you. I'd slap you, but you're my best friend and I just can't."

"You can stop now," I replied.

"Okay. Now, are you going to go out there and kiss the living shit out of your hunk?"

Biting my bottom lip, I shook my head. Manda swore and started reaching for me again. I backed up.

"Wait, I have an excuse."

"Oh, this had better be good. You two have been texting each other for over a month. I've seen some of the texts." I glared. "Well, your phone was just lying there while you got ready. Anyway, my point is, the texts I read were pure flirtation. You two are hot for one another. You have been your whole life."

"I haven't told him about Switch."

"Fuck," she whispered. Manda knew everything, and I meant everything. Before she came back to Caroline Springs, I filled her in on Jerimiah and me. How he wanted more from me and how hesitant I was because of Python. She told me I was crazy of course. Though I just hadn't mentioned to Manda I'd been putting off telling Jerimiah how his father drove me out of town. At first, I hadn't wanted to leave, but then Blackie had advised it because it would also protect Jerimiah.

Manda shook her head. "Doesn't matter. He won't care... in the end, and then you both can get the grind on." She thrust her hips back and forth. Then stopped. "Seriously, Poppy. Your man is a goner for you. I can't see the news of Switch fucking it up between you two."

"Jerimiah told me... he said, he thought I could have been his forever. Even back when we were in high school. I don't want to rush this if we're each other's future forever."

Her expression softened. "Honey, how could it be rushing when really you've both been in love with each other for like a billion years already?"

I snorted. "I didn't love him until grade ten at least, and then I left at the end of the year."

Manda raised her brows at me and crossed her arms over her chest.

"I didn't."

She rolled her eyes.

Throwing my hands up, I then let them fall to my sides, and said, "Okay, maybe I was a little in like with him, but it wasn't love."

"Sure. Okay, uh-huh. We'll talk about that lie later. What you need to do now is have private time with your man and tell him the final piece of the puzzle."

Shifting my gaze to the mirror, I could see the bruise under my make-up. "What happens when Python comes back and harms more people in Jerimiah's life?"

Manda stepped in front of me. "Can't you see by now he doesn't care about the danger? Even his brothers don't care. What they care about is keeping you safe... for Fang. They'd take on the world for you because of him, and Fang would do anything, risk anything, to have you at his side."

I closed my eyes to hold back the tears. She was right, but maybe I just couldn't understand the why of it. What made me so special to have Jerimiah's love? For all of them to have my back in this situation? Sucking in a deep breath, I opened my eyes and nodded.

If they saw worth in me, then the only thing I could do was cherish it, appreciate it, and take care of what they were offering. A new family. With the man I had always loved.

Manda took my hands and beamed a bright smile right at me. "Yay, let's get out there so you can claim what's yours, and I'll keep that lush Muff occupied while you do it." She clapped and spun towards the door.

Quickly, I grabbed her arm. "Manda, you've just moved back. I'm not sure Muff is the type of guy for you. I heard he gets around a lot."

She giggled. "Honey, I'm not looking to date, but a little flirting and heavy petting won't go astray. Hell, I might even add in dry humping he's just that fine."

Scoffing, I shook my head at my best friend, but I did it smiling. God, I'd missed having her around. We'd kept in contact when I'd left and never stopped. However, contact through emails, texts, and phone calls just hadn't been the same. To have her with me, and in the flesh, was amazing.

We waded our way through the people back to the bar where Jerimiah was having intense words with Muff. When he saw us approaching, he said something quickly and then stepped back.

Poor Muff looked like a lost little puppy when he eyed Manda as she sat back in her seat.

"Sorry about that, took longer than it should have. Muff, would you care to dance?"

Muff's eyes popped wide. He glanced from Jerimiah and then back to Manda. His jaw clenched. "Baby, I don't dance, but I could come watch you shake it and keep the other fuckers away."

Manda smiled. "Sounds great to me."

"Muff," Jerimiah warned low.

"Cool it, brother. I ain't a dick. When a lady asks me, I won't deny her."

They walked off towards the dance floor. I choked on a sip of my wine when Manda started grinding her hips around and around, while running her hands all over her body. Muff's gaze heated, until he looked back to Jerimiah. Muff quickly schooled his features and then stood there with his legs planted apart and his arms crossed over his chest. When another guy started to get close to

Manda, Muff barked at them to back off. The way his face screwed up would scare many, so it was no surprise when the guy fled.

Since Jerimiah was still watching Muff, no doubt because he'd warned his brother away from Manda and that was probably because he was worried about me in a roundabout way, I reached up and laid my hand on his chest.

His eyes swung down to me. Grinning, I said, "Don't worry about Manda. She can take care of herself. Besides, I've already told her to stay away from Muff. I'd heard he was a player, but the look on her face said she didn't care at all."

"If he fucks her over—"

"It won't be an issue between us. They're grown-ups. They can handle it."

He studied my face to see how serious I was. Jerimiah nodded, lifted his head and shifted his gaze over to his brother. Turning, I watched first Jerimiah nod at Muff, then Muff's bright smile before he moved in and wrapped his arms around Manda, pulling her close and swaying with her.

"Darlin'," Jerimiah's voice was soft, his eyes were just as soft, "I'm gonna kiss you now."

My body jolted. "What? Why?"

He chuckled. "Because I want to, and you want me to."

Glaring, I said, "You're very sure of yourself."

"Yeah." He winked.

"Then maybe next time you shouldn't tell me and freak me out, just do it."

He shifted closer, grabbed my knees and widened them so he could step between them.

I forgot how to breathe.

"I'll have to remember you prefer sneak attacks." He grinned, and it was totally cocky.

"Jerimiah, I—" Movement caught my attention, and I froze. My eyes widened when they landed on who it was.

No, no, no. Not here. Not now.

Oh God… Oh God…. I watched as he raised his hand and pointed his finger at the back of Jerimiah's head. He motioned his fingers like a gun. His lips moved, and I knew what he'd mouthed.

Bang.

Python was in the Hawks MC bar and threatening to shoot Jerimiah. Terror clutched at my heart. He'd already done enough. Couldn't he just leave me alone?

In a blink, he disappeared, but I got his message. I got it.

He didn't want me around the Hawks. Especially Jerimiah or he'd kill them.

"Poppy!" Jerimiah's hands landed on my face. "Darlin', what is it?"

Frantically, my eyes roamed over his face. I couldn't lose him.

Not when I'd just got him back.

"Poppy?"

"What's going on?" Manda asked from beside us.

"Brother?" Muff said.

"Tell me, darlin'," Jerimiah pressed.

He needed to protect himself. Concentrate on him, his family, and not me.

The thought that there was a chance of losing him hacked at my heart and soul.

"H-he was just here," I whispered.

Jerimiah straightened to his full height. He moved this and that way, looking to find him. "Fuck," he snarled. "Christ. He was here, in Pick's bar, on Hawks territory." He gripped my wrist and pulled me off my seat. "Can you still see him?"

"No. He's gone."

"Shit, okay." He nodded. "Pick," he called. "Keys, office."

"You good?" I heard him ask.

"Yeah, brother."

I noticed Muff crowded Manda after hearing what we'd said. He was also searching the place. I heard a jangle of keys, and then Jerimiah led me away from the bar, down the hallway, where the toilets were, to the end where he unlocked a door.

He ushered me through, releasing my hand. I stepped

in, a few paces away and turned to find Manda and Muff had followed.

Manda came right up to me, guiding me to the desk where she shifted things so I could sit because I wasn't sure my legs could hold me up much longer.

CHAPTER FIFTEEN

FANG

*A*fter closing the door, I stalked over to the desk, then gently shifted Manda outta the way and got close to my woman. Tipping her head back with a finger under her chin, I said, "Darlin', it's going to be okay."

She blinked as if she'd forgotten where she was, lost in her mind. "He was *here*." She swallowed, and it looked like it hurt. She shook her head, tears welling. "He was here, Jerimiah. In a Hawks bar without a care in the world, and did this to you." She made a gesture with her hand. A gun and being shot at me.

"He won't get to me," I stated, cupping the side of her

cheek. "Darlin', he won't get to me." The motherfucker may have had balls to come into Hawks territory and threaten a brother *with his hand*, but he wasn't stupid enough to actually pull a gun out surrounded by brothers. He would have been taken down to the ground in seconds. But hell, I was still fuckin' pissed he'd managed to get in through the door. Something we'd have to take into account and deal with. Though, comforting my woman was my main concern.

"Baby, I need you to tell me absolutely everything that happened between you and him. Why would he still be after you?"

Poppy licked her dry lips. "I don't know. I don't understand it."

"He's been threatening to fuck her though," Manda added.

"Manda," Poppy snapped.

"They have to know everything. He still wants her," she looked at me, "but he's claimed her—" She cleared her throat. "—pussy as his, like he's already claimed her as his woman. So he wants no one else near her."

Straightening, Poppy's hands fell from my face, landing on my waist where she ran them up and down. I would have snorted if I wasn't fuming. My woman was trying to calm me. So for her sake, I closed my eyes and breathed deeply through my nose.

"Muff, you're coming with me. We're gonna swing by

the compound for Gamer, then pay Venom a visit." I wanted to talk to Blackie, make sure he was telling us everything.

My eyes opened when Poppy suddenly gripped my tee at the waist, and yelled, "What? No! Python is a sick fuck. Hell, he's probably there just to mess with Blackie. It won't be safe. I have a plan. If I just stay away from you all, long enough for him to forget about me, then—"

"No," I clipped. "We don't play by his rules. Not after everything he's done. We play by ours, and I will not fuckin' have you outta my life because of him. We'll make Python see reason." After we break him first.

"Jerimiah, it won't be for that long—"

"Four years was enough without you. Not again," I ordered. Hell, didn't she understand I'd never let her walk away from me? Maybe from the way her eyes were warming and brimming with tears she was finally getting it.

Her breath hitched. "I-I'm already losing my mum. I won't lose you or hurt anyone else in your family."

Crushed.

My goddamn heart was just crushed by the pain in Poppy's voice.

Stepping close, I wrapped my arms around her. She buried her head into my chest, her body shaking with her falling tears. Fuck me.

"Poppy," I whispered softly. "I promise I'll be fine,

nothing will happen to me. No more harm will come to me or my brothers. You gotta trust that. Trust me and the Hawks."

She shook her head against me. "But you can't promise that."

"I can. Fuck this guy, Poppy. Fuck him. My woman doesn't deserve this type of treatment, especially when she's already going through enough. And if I can deal with it, get the bad outta your life, then I will. Promise, Poppy, I'll be good. Everyone will be fine. I know it because I'll have my brothers at my back."

"I-I'm not even your woman." The words trembled out of her. I felt the urge to shake my bloody woman. Instead, I dropped my head back, eyes to the ceiling, and prayed for fuckin' patience. Poppy Torian had been mine since the day we'd become friends. We lost what we had, but then she became mine once again the day she opened the door to me in a towel.

"Come on, baby. We'll wait for them out front," Muff said to Manda, and I heard them move within the room, then step out the door. As soon as I heard it close, I slide my hands from around Poppy's shoulders to the top of her arms, so I could pull her back and capture her eyes.

She wiped at her face, smearing her eye make-up a little, but I didn't give a flying fuck. She was gorgeous no matter what.

When more tears fell, it gutted me. I hadn't seen much

of the agony she'd been in over her mother. She'd been holding it back and I'd been blind to it. I should have known. Fuck, I *should* have known. She was losing her mum. Wiping under her eyes, I leaned in and pressed my lips to her forehead.

"Fuck, Poppy," I whispered, then pulled back.

"What?" she sniffed.

"I should have come for you. I should have shoved my pride and pain aside and found you all those years ago. Then, hell, none of this would have happened, and we'd be where I want us now. You'd be mine, and I could have helped you deal with the pain you're already feeling for your mum." Closing my eyes for a moment, I took a breath and opened them again. "I'm sorry, babe."

Christ. Her bottom lip wobbled. "S-she doesn't remember me some days. I never thought my mum could forget me. W-when I walk in there and she looks at me like I just work there..." She grabbed her chest. "...it hurts. Like I've been stabbed right here each and every time."

Nodding, I cupped her cheek. "Darlin', fuck, let me be it." Her body stiffened. "I'm not sayin' your man. I ain't forcing us on you. I'm asking to be the one you turn to, when that pain gets too much and you can't deal, call me, text me, or come to me, and let me help you with what you're feeling. That's all I'm askin', sweetheart."

She studied me for a moment, before she whispered,

"There's something else I have to tell you before you want to be anything with me." Reaching up, she took my hand from her face in both of hers and brought it to her lap. There she absently ran her fingers over the back of my hand while thoughts ran around in her mind.

Of course I was wondering what she had to say, but I wouldn't rush her. Whatever it was seemed important. Shit, maybe this was why—

"This is the other reason I left." She looked up, licking her lips. "I-if you… I'll understand if you don't want anything to do with me after it."

My body tensed. The reason would have me backing off Poppy?

What the fuck?

"Tell me," I said, and it came out gruffer than I'd meant it to. So, I gripped one of her hands in mine and brought both our hands to my chest where I laid hers flat on my chest with my hand over hers. Our gazes met. "I'm sure whatever it is I'll never risk losing you again."

She tried to tug her hand away, but I wouldn't let it drop. She sighed, wiped at her face again, and then muttered, "We'll see." Taking a breath, she looked up at me, and said, "The night I overheard what you'd said, I went back to the compound to… let's just say, I wanted to drink my teen sorrows away. Hardly anyone was around. I snuck into the fridge out back to grab myself some beers when…." She looked away, biting her bottom lip. "I should have told you, but I was so angry and hurt and worried about what you would do." She sniffed. "Switch came in after me," she whispered. My body went rock solid. When her gaze flicked down to her hands, I looked there to see I was gripping so tightly the tips of her fingers were turning white. I released them, then stepped back.

Switch got to her.

Turning my back to her, I snarled, "Did he fuckin' touch you?"

I waited a beat for her to deny it, but she didn't. Fury rose once again. That time I had to let it out. I had to let it fuckin' free. Picking up a chair, I threw it at the wall. It smashed, but it wasn't enough.

Just when I'd picked up something else, the door came open.

"Fang, what the fuck?" Muff barked.

With a heaving breath, I placed the item on the ground. "Get out," I ordered darkly.

"Brother?"

"Poppy, you okay?" Manda asked.

"Get the fuck out," I snarled.

"Switch...," I heard Manda mumble. She knew. She fuckin' knew, and I hadn't. For years. Goddamn years I didn't know my fucked-up, motherfuckin' cunt of a father touched my woman. I hadn't been there to protect her. I'd been too consumed with my own petty worries about Poppy being too young and wanting her but had been too horny and stupid to claim my woman like I should have, no matter her age. I shouldn't have waited. Then she wouldn't have been hurt and tried to drown her pain, *and then* she wouldn't have been touched. Instead, she would have been by my fucking side.

My fucking father got his hands on her.

Gripping my hair, it built the pain, wrath... so much built inside of me. Bending over, I let it out. I roared into the room until I felt her.

Poppy was at my back, her hands on my waist, holding tight. Her voice only a dull sound, one I couldn't hear right because my ears were ringing.

Crouching, I held my head in my hands. Poppy's warmth wrapped over my back. I didn't understand how she thought I wouldn't want to be with her after, but she was wrong. *I'd* fucked up. It was *my* fault what had happened to her. Not hers.

"Jerimiah, please, please listen. He only got a hand down my pants. That was it. Then Blackie found us and got me out of there. Blackie warned me you would lose it, probably kill Switch. *I* knew you would. There was no probably about it. You were always so protective of me. I didn't want you to go to jail for me. To kill your father for me. So I left."

She shifted back when I stood.

Scrubbing at my face, I turned to her. "You were

right." She stiffened, her lips parted. "I would have killed him. No matter how far he got, it doesn't matter. He put his hands on you, scared you. He would have paid with his life. But, Poppy..." I sighed, running a hand through my hair. "That's the way I work. How the club works. You have to understand that. We hunt, we hurt and kill those who fuck us over. And I mean goddamn us as in our family. No matter who it is in the family, we all come together to make them pay. Blackie fucked up. He should have told me so I could've made Switch disappear a long time ago. I wouldn't have been locked up for it, Poppy. Not for that sick cunt. I get why you ran. You went through a lot that night, yet, you were still looking out for me. I failed you. I wouldn't have lost you, and that wouldn't have happened to you if I'd stepped the fuck up and claimed you."

She stepped closer. Her hands once again gripped my tee, only to loosen one hand and slide it up to the side of my neck. "Please don't. Please, *do not* blame yourself. You warned me away from the compound without you there *and* from him. I didn't listen. I should have listened."

"Don't, darlin'. This is on me. You can't make me see different, but what you can do, if you want to, is forgive me."

She glared. My stubborn woman wouldn't let me take it on. Her hand squeezed my neck. "I don't need to forgive you for anything."

"Baby, you do, but I get it if you can't."

Poppy let out a cute little growl in the back of her throat. Fuck me. I'd fucked us up and he'd got to her. It'd live with me forever. All I could do was pray I could make everything up to her. Pray she'd let me.

"Okay." She nodded. "You're forgiven."

Placing my hands to her hips, I applied pressure for a second so I had her attention. "Darlin', you can't just—"

"I can offer my forgiveness when I want, and I'm saying I forgive you, Jerimiah. Now take it, and then you can take mine for leaving."

Narrowing my gaze, I clipped, "I'm not taking yours when you have nothing to be sorry for. Jesus, Poppy, I—" I didn't get to finish because a certain someone shut me up by placing her lips on mine.

At first touch, I was a goner.

Christ, as soon as she wrapped both her arms around my neck, I curled mine around her waist and picked her up off the floor. Poppy brought up her legs around my hips. My hands went right to her arse. Her sweet arse. To hold her close while deepening the kiss. When she moaned, after opening for me, I turned us and walked her back to the desk, planting her on it so my hands could roam freely over her hot body.

Too soon she was ending it. I didn't like it. With a grunted growl, I shook my head, our lips sliding against one another before tangling my tongue with hers once again. She responded with a whimper, tightening her legs around me, forcing me into her more.

I couldn't get enough, and neither could Poppy because she was more than willing to keep the kiss going.

Jesus. I was rock hard in my jeans.

From a kiss.

My dick throbbed from one kiss from my woman. It didn't bode well for our first night together. I'd probably come from just seeing her naked.

Oh hell, the thought of Poppy naked had me leaking into my boxers. With my hands going back to her arse, I slid her forward, holding close. There was no way she was disappearing right then.

Love.

This was what it was.

The kiss was love and longing and desire all wrapped into one.

Shit, fuck. I should have done it a long time ago. Her lips, her mouth… were more than I'd ever dreamed of, and I'd dreamed, fantasised a lot about our first kiss.

She was made for me, and there was no way in hell I was losing her.

When my nipple was suddenly put under a vice and squeezed hard, I broke the kiss, snapping, "What the hell?"

"Air, I needed air," Poppy panted. Her hand went to her heart as she took in gulps of oxygen.

Rubbing my nipple, I asked, "You could have just told me?"

She snorted, then giggled. "Sorry, I was enjoying it too much. My body talked before I could."

"Christ, woman." It still stung.

"Sorry." She blushed when her gaze landed on my mouth. "I kissed you," she whispered, more to herself, probably realising the kiss was real and hell yes, it had been. My dick was still reliving it. Even after the wench twisted my nipple.

"You did." I smirked.

"You know I did it to shut you up, right?"

"I do, but I don't give a fuck. You can shut me up anytime you want like that."

Her blush deepened down to her neck. Cute.

"Um…" She licked her lips, her eyes landing back on my mouth. I stepped closer, and her hand came up. "So, can we, ah, say that we both forgive each other and move on?"

I clenched my jaw. I wasn't sure I'd ever forgive myself, but I had to give her what she wanted to hear. "Sure."

With a scowl, she crossed her arms over her chest, and said, "That *sure* sounds like you're just appeasing me."

Raising my brows, I smirked. "Sure."

She growled under her breath. Her hand came out

ready to smack me, but I grabbed it. I tugged her until she came off the desk and into my arms.

"Darlin', I'll try, okay. I'll try to forgive myself, but it'll take time. As long as I know I have you at my side, I *could* make it work."

"You do," she whispered. "Have me at your side."

"Good." I grinned. "So there'll be no more talk about you not being my woman. It's happened. You're mine, I'm yours, and none of it means we have to rush anything. But what it does mean is that I protect what's mine. I'm dealin' with that fucker Python. You with me?"

She sucked in a ragged breath and nodded. "Yes."

Fuckin' finally.

Poppy was mine.

Like I'd told her, I wasn't risking rushing this, us. I'd take each day as it came as long as Poppy was there.

Christ. I felt like screaming the room down with my elation. Shit, I'd even do my own dance of happiness if I didn't have things to do.

"I gotta get you and Manda home, then head off. Want Manda stayin' with you tonight. No ifs or buts." She rolled her eyes, and I chuckled. "Know you want to argue. Any other time I'd go head to head with you for the fun of it, but not now. Not when I gotta get my woman safe."

"Try to keep the Hulk at bay so I don't have to visit you in jail."

I scoffed. "Baby, when're you gonna learn? I'd never

go to jail. Hawks have cops at our back. If they knew my reasoning, they'd understand and protect me. All of us."

"Okay… I think. Just stay safe, Jerimiah."

"I will. You gonna give me more about your mum tomorrow night?"

She tensed, then relaxed and ran her hands up and down my arms. "I-I… um… yes."

Closing my eyes for a second, I opened them, leaned in and touched my mouth to hers. She sighed, a content one, which of course I fuckin' liked.

"So you won't be dodging me anymore?"

She laughed. "I won't."

"Good. Let's get goin', yeah?"

Heat hit her cheeks. "After one more," she said, eyeing my lips.

I grinned like a lovesick fool. She shifted closer, her lips an inch away from mine. There I murmured, "I'm all yours, darlin'."

CHAPTER SIXTEEN

FANG

With my woman on the back of my bike, and Muff following Manda as she drove her car back, we arrived at Poppy's. After I parked, I climbed off my ride after Poppy.

She removed the helmet, glanced at the house, then back to me. "I thought you had to get going?"

Smirking, I shook my head and watched as Manda parked in the drive, while Muff pulled up behind me. "Did you honestly think I wouldn't let Charlie know what's goin' down?"

"Don't you dare!" she snapped low. "He's going through enough. He doesn't need to know this."

"Know what?" Charlie asked from behind his daughter, causing her to jump.

I'd seen him come from the house just as Muff turned off his ride. Poppy had been too pissed to notice.

Poppy spun, smiled, and then moved forward to turn her father around, trying to usher him inside. "Nothing, Dad. Everything's fine. Hey, Manda has decided to stay the night. How about we play some cards?"

"Yeah, Mr Torian, that sounds like a good idea." Manda took Charlie's arm, and like the good friend she was, she tried to help Poppy get him inside. They managed a couple of steps.

"Girls," Charlie bit out.

They stopped. Manda dropped her hands, and Poppy threw hers up. "Fine. Find out what's going on, but don't blame me if the stress gets to you, and then you eat through it, turning into a beach ball."

Charlie snorted. He faced his girl and tucked a stray piece of hair behind her ear. He'd read the fear from his daughter and reassured her with, "Honey, I'll be fine. Promise I'm not going anywhere, no matter how much comes our way. I'm a strong sucker. Stronger than I look or my age shows." After Poppy nodded, he took her hand in his and looked to me. "What's going on?"

"Python," I said, and the fucker's name had Charlie tensing, his face becoming guarded. "He was at the bar tonight. Freaked Poppy out. Threatened my life."

"Jesus," Charlie muttered.

"I'm heading to see Blackie, see if he's holding anything back."

"He won't be."

"I gotta make sure, Charlie. Need to protect what's mine."

Charlie asked a question that had me grinning. "So," he drew out, "you two together now?"

"Dad!" Poppy cried, her face heating at her father's question. "Seriously? All you're worried about is if Jerimiah and I are together?"

He shrugged and glanced back to me. Chuckling, I nodded. "She's mine, always has been."

Poppy huffed. "I don't get you two. Are you not worried about Python?"

Charlie shook his head. "Fang has it covered. Things'll be fine."

"That's it? Jerimiah has it covered and you don't need to worry?"

He grinned. "Well, yeah. He's protected you for years back in the day. I never had to worry then, so I know I don't need to now."

She moved her eyes from her dad to me, to her dad, and then they returned to me. "I should have known once Jerimiah was on the case, Dad could handle anything."

"Yep." I grinned, and she glared back.

"Fine. Go off and be a superhero. But if you come back with so much as a scratch, I'll hurt you myself."

My grin grew. "Look forward to it."

"Dad," Poppy said quietly, while she watched me.

"Yes, honey?"

"I'm going to say bye to Jerimiah. You might want to go inside for this next part," she replied, and then made her way over to me.

"Shit" was all Charlie said, before I heard his footsteps heading towards the house.

I didn't take my eyes away from Poppy… until I heard, "Do I get a kiss goodbye too?" My eyes sliced to Muff. Whatever he saw from my expression had his hands coming up in front of him. "I didn't mean from your woman."

Poppy's hand on the side of my face turned my head back towards her. Then everything was forgotten, but the feel of her lips on mine.

WE'D TRADED our rides at the compound for Muff's four-wheel drive, and picked Gamer up.

On the ride to Venom's compound, I made a call to Parker and explained what I needed.

"Yeah, brother. I'll do the search and find him," he reassured, after I told him what I learned.

"Appreciate it," I said. "When or if you get the information, you let me know first. No one else."

"Fang, you sure that's wise?"

"I won't be stupid. I'll have my brothers with me when I get to him."

"I'll be coming too."

"Parker—"

"Fuck no, Fang. I'm coming. Someone in the law needs to have you covered."

Christ. Parker and Lan, even though they were with the law, being detectives, it was a bonus to have them around the club. Not only that, they'd proved themselves to us and were brothers in every goddamn way. If Parker wanted to have my back when I hunted my mother-fuckin' father and made sure he no longer breathed, then he could.

"Brother" was all I said. What he said meant something to me.

"Talk soon," he replied, his tone light, so I knew he understood that his offer meant something.

"Yeah," I said, hanging up.

"Parker won't be the only one who comes with you," Gamer commented from the back of the car. Muff grunted in agreement. "You'll need to inform Dodge," Gamer added.

"I will." I nodded.

"How you think your woman will handle it?" Muff

asked.

"Didn't know you had a woman until that phone call, brother," Gamer mentioned.

"Her name's Poppy. A woman from my past, but she's now my future."

He hummed. "Sweet, when do I get to meet her?"

"Soon. And to answer your question, Muff, she'll understand." He snorted. I laughed in response. "Okay, eventually. We need to find Python first though."

"Fuck yes," Muff agreed.

"You know none of us will hold you back, even though he's your dad," Gamer said, just as we pulled up out front of the Venom clubhouse.

"Good. Thanks, brothers."

Blackie had installed new gates out front and a control panel to talk into it. Didn't mean we didn't ignore the members strolling along the fence guarding it. One spotted us and before we could say a word, the gates opened. Could be worried we'd slam through them in our vehicle like Stoke and Vicious had the last time they paid Blackie a visit. I'd been on the other side of the fence then, a patched-in Venom, but I was feeding all the information I could to the Hawks. Not that Hawks had asked me to, they hadn't, and even told me it was a stupid move since Parker—not that I knew at the time—was undercover on the inside of Venom too.

Shit, it seemed like decades ago that happened, but it'd

only been about two years and now I had Hawks blood running through me. All the way through me, to the core. I respected the club and all we stood for. Venom's creed had been sketchy from the start.

"Fang," Rattle, a member I knew when I was Venom, greeted. I waited for the look of disdain, only surprisingly, it never came. Most of the members hated me after snitching on them to Hawks. Rattle had been one of them. "What the fuck you doin' here, traitor?" His voice was low, harsh, but didn't match the neutral look on his face. Rattle stopped right in front of me, causing my brothers to crowd my back. He glanced at them quickly, a cocky smirk landing on his lips. "You boys think you can take me?"

"There's no thinkin' involved," Muff said.

Rattle was a few years older than Muff, who was thirty-two. He was a big bastard and would try his best at taking us on, but he'd lose.

"Just here to talk to Blackie, Rattle."

More Venom members came outta the cracks to see what was goin' on. Takin' *their* brother's back. "You ain't walkin' through that door until you tell me what you want."

Jaw clenched, I snarled, "You suddenly get patched into a higher rank? I don't need to say shit to you. Get Blackie."

"We don't take orders from scum like you."

"Fuckin' hell, these wankers serious?" Muff said.

"You need to shut up."

Muff stepped up, got in Rattle's face. "No. You need to shut the fuck up and get who we want to deal with. And if any of you motherfuckers mouth off to a brother of Hawks again, you'll be askin' for it. Shit, your own prez was smart enough to give over the men in your club because they were in cahoots with Baxter. Now we got yet another situation, and it involves one of yours. He took blood from Hawks. *No one* fucks with Hawks. So you need to get over Fang helpin' us out since he did it for the right reasons. To save lives. No one was crossed by him in your club who shouldn't have been, and you know it."

When silence was the answer to Muff's speech, which I kinda got a heart-swell from since he was taking my back in that way, Gamer announced loudly, "Enough of this standin' around trying to measure whose dick is bigger." That brought a few chuckles around.

"Rattle, step back," Blackie called from the compound doorway.

"Oh, it's my sweet, sweet boy" was cried from behind Blackie, and then Roda, Blackie's woman, who he glared and shook his head at, pushed past him and ran our way.

"What the fuck?" Muff muttered.

"Huh, guess all clubs have some crazy women," Gamer commented, just as Roda collided with me. Her arms circled around my waist. Only she didn't stop there. She pulled back, grinned up at me, planted both her hands on my cheeks and brought me in for a quick kiss. She pushed me back, glared, and then slapped my face. The force of it stung. But I should have been expecting it. When Poppy left town, Blackie and Roda's place became like a second home to me. I used to hang there all the time. Their girls were all younger than Poppy and me and had become like sisters to me. I hadn't seen them recently.

"Roda." I groaned in frustration.

"What, you think you're too good to see your second momma? My boy forgets about us and we don't see him for months, Fang. *Months*. You had better have a good explanation, young man."

"Woman, get your arse in here," Blackie called.

Roda spun. "Don't you woman me. You know, you've listened to me every night complain about our boy not having time for us."

"Fuck me," Blackie cursed, thumping his forehead with his palm. Some of the Venom members dissipated, chuckling, used to the drama Roda brought. Everyone loved her though; she was a momma to all of us, no matter the age. That was even before Blackie became president. "Fang, get in here, and maybe she'll calm the hell down."

Starting for the door, Muff and Gamer followed, but

Roda turned her attention to Rattle. I glanced to see her get close to him and start hissing. His head dropped back, eyes to the stars, and he sighed heavily.

"And I thought Low was bad. She ain't nothin' compared to that," Muff whispered.

Gamer laughed. "Maybe they should meet…." He trailed off when we both glared at him. "Yeah, okay, that would not be wise."

"Ya think?" Muff shook his head.

"Son, what'ya doin' here?" Blackie asked, shifting aside for us to enter.

"Need a word in private, Blackie."

"Shit," he bit out. "I've already told Dodge everything about Python."

"Want a word, Blackie."

He sighed. "Back room."

As we made our way through the common area, we got a few stares. I took them all in, meeting all their cold gazes and returned them with my own before Blackie led us down a short hall to the door at the end.

He entered. We followed, Gamer closing the door behind us. Blackie went around the desk and sat, then gestured to the seats opposite, but I shook my head.

"We won't be here long," I stated.

His brows raised. "What's goin' on?"

"Python came into our business. I didn't see him or

catch him, but Poppy was there. She saw it all, freaked her out big time."

He tensed. "Fuck. She okay?"

I shook my head. I was gonna play dirty. "I thought she was a mess the night I got to her after the shooting, but tonight, the amount of fear I saw in her was worse than the night I held her crying in my arms. She's losing her ma, Blackie. You know this, and then to top it off, she has this shit to deal with from that motherfucker. When he threatened me, she lost it."

Worry washed over his face before he sighed and ran a hand over the back of his neck. Blackie leaned forward, arms going to the desk. "I gave Dodge everything, Fang." His jaw clenched. "But..." I froze from that one word. "I didn't want it to come to this. Thought you'd have your hands on him by now. Didn't know he'd be this slippery. I have his momma's address."

Jesus Christ.

"He see her a lot?" Gamer asked.

"As far as I know, yeah." He eyed us all slowly. "Want our Poppy safe, so I'd do anything to make sure it happens." He pulled open his drawer, put his hand in, then up, and slapped something to his desk. "You need to take a few of my men. Poppy's Venom—"

"Poppy's Hawks business now, Blackie. She's mine. So no one but Hawks on this trip."

His eyes widened right before he threw back his

head and laughed. Bending forward, a hand planted on his desk. "Ah, shit. Goddamn." He shook his head, grinning. "About bloody time. You two've been hot for each other for far too long. Well, until she went away—"

Leaning in, I touched my fisted knuckles to his desk. "Yeah, that's something we'll talk about soon."

His jaw clenched. "You know?"

"Found out tonight."

"You know you've been like a son to me, so you have to understand why I suggested for her to go."

Christ. I did.

"Doesn't mean we couldn't have taken him out together."

Blackie shook his head. "It wasn't the right time. It would have been you, me, and Charlie against the rest. They didn't see him for who he was until later. You know that."

I snarled, "I lost her for *four* fuckin' years because of him. So she could protect *me*."

"You were both young, and shit, look at it now. It's worked out."

"You're lucky it has."

He tipped his chair back. "You'd better get your arse, and Poppy's, to our house soon for dinner or Roda is gonna skin you both alive. Though, when she finds out you two are together, you might get some forgiveness.

She's gonna be fuckin' thrilled. Means my night could end happy."

Shaking my head, I straightened. "Jesus, Blackie. Too much information."

"Boy, I may be old, but I still know how to use my big black dick."

Muff laughed outright, Gamer chuckled, and I goddamn groaned. Holding out my hand, I clicked my fingers. "Just give me the fuckin' address."

He picked it up and offered it to me. Before I could take it, he snatched it back. "Dinner?"

"Right." I nodded.

"I'm gonna tell Roda you're with Poppy."

"Don't care who you tell. In fact, tell every goddamn person you know she's off limits." I glared, then snatched the paper outta his hand.

Blackie chuckled. Only it died when I met his gaze. "What?" he asked.

"You should know I'm goin' after him and takin' him out."

"Switch?" he snarled.

"Yeah. Soon as I get the information on where he's at."

"Want in on that, Fang."

"Again, it's Hawks business."

He shook his head. "And Venom's. You won't let me help with Poppy's shit, but you gotta let me in on this, brother. Got a lot of regret on how things were handled.

The biggest was that I never slit that motherfucker's throat. Want at your back when it's goin' down."

Fuck. I stared at the man who'd always managed to draw a laugh from me when I'd been down after Poppy left, the man who'd sat there and listened to my shit whenever I needed him to. The man who had me, and sometimes my ma, in his house and at his table on so many times I'd lost count. Yeah, we'd both fucked up: him not telling me about Poppy and what he knew, and me not having his back when he needed it the most as he took over as president.

Shit. Blackie was family even if a different club ran through our veins.

Giving him a chin lift, I said, "I'll get in touch."

The relief was noticeable when his shoulders dropped. "Appreciate it, brother."

Behind us, we heard a sniffle.

Turning, I rolled my eyes at Roda standing quietly in the doorway. Not sure how long she'd been there. She whimpered, "You and Poppy?" She threw herself at me again, wrapping her arms around my neck, and burying her face against me. "I'm so happy," she cried. She pulled back and glared up at me. "But you make sure you bring our girl to dinner soon, and your momma."

"Will do, Roda." I patted her back and eased her away when Blackie came around and claimed her around her neck, pulling her into him.

"Talk soon," he said.

"Very soon," Roda added.

"Will do." I nodded, and left with Muff and Gamer.

On the way out, Gamer laughed. "Not sure I ever want a woman. Bitches be crazy, at least the ones I've met."

"Not all," Muff said. "I want one, and I have my eye—" I shot him a glance. "Ah, never mind."

"You screw Manda over we'll have problems."

"And if she screws me over? You gonna be all protective for your brother?"

Shit. Was I?

"Suppose."

"You love me," he cooed. I smacked him up the back of the head.

"Get your head back in the game."

"Always is when we need to deliver some pain to make a point for Hawks," he said before climbing into the car.

That was true. We may mess around a lot, but when it came to crunch time, we'd be 100 percent there and involved in the situation.

CHAPTER SEVENTEEN

POPPY

"*P*oppy." My name was whispered above me. "Poppy." It was a little louder, and this time came with a poke to my cheek. "Poppy!" was shouted right in my face.

"Go the hell away," I moaned, and then slowly opened my eyes, to only close them again. "That is not a sight I wish to wake up to, Manda. Cover them up."

"Oh, oops." She giggled.

"Is it safe?" I asked, rubbing my face.

"Yes. The girls are put away, ready to fall out for another day."

"Thank God." With my hands pressed to the mattress,

I slid back, resting against the bedhead, and then reached for my phone. "Damn," I muttered when I activated it and saw there was no text from Jerimiah. My eyes widened. "It's nearly 1:00 p.m? Why didn't anyone wake me?"

"Ah, that's what I was doing." Manda rolled her eyes. She went over to my drawers, grabbed a jumper and pulled it over her head to cover her singlet top. "Can't have the girls making an appearance in front of Charlie."

"So you haven't been up that long?"

"No, I've been up for ages. But Charlie was still in bed until just before. I think everyone needed a sleep in."

"I should get dressed, go see Mum with him to keep my mind off… things."

"He's going to be okay. You know that, right?"

"Yes." I nodded. I did know it because I refused to think otherwise. Besides, Jerimiah would do anything to make sure he came back to me in one piece, or I'd kill him myself. After folding back my covers, I got out of bed and stretched. My glance to my phone didn't go unnoticed though.

"He'll text or call as soon as he's got information, Poppy."

Groaning, I nodded. "I know this, but it doesn't make me not worry."

"I know." She smiled sadly. "How about we go see your mum and then take Charlie out after for a very late lunch slash early dinner?"

"Sounds good."

After showering, I dressed in jeans and a simple navy tee then made my way into the living room... only to stop.

"W-what's going on?"

Dad looked up from having his head buried in his hands. Tears ran down his cheeks.

No. I shook my head.

Manda stood. I backed up.

No. My hands came up to ward her off.

Dad also stood. "Poppy." His voice hitched.

No. I bit my bottom lip.

"I-it's your mum, honey."

No!

Tears filled my eyes. My whole body shuddered with the breath I took. Manda made it to me, her arm coming around me, and she guided me to my dad. The whole time I pushed back against her arm. My heart cracked. My chest ached. I didn't want it to break.

I wouldn't handle it.

"Honey, t-they found her this morning. S-she managed to get her hands on... on some drugs." He choked on the words, cleared his throat and then tried his best to go on with his voice thick. "T-they didn't want to t-tell us on the phone." He sniffed. His hands went to my shoulders. Fresh tears fell from his eyes. "People from the home d-dropped in... s-she...." He groaned deep in this throat, then grunted out through a sob caught there.

I begged in my mind, *No, no, no. Please, not Mum.*

"M-my moon left us some letters."

"I-I can't," I managed to get out.

"No." He shook his head. "I know, not now. God, not now."

I sniffed, looking away from the agony etched into his face, and took a shuddering breath. "S-she's gone."

Manda's arm around me convulsed. I knew she was crying while trying to hold me together, hold us together.

Dad's pained wail of "Yes," was what broke me.

Falling forward, I screamed into my father's chest. I sobbed, cried, and yelled. Manda buried in, while Dad buried into both of us. We all held one another as we let the anguish take over.

FANG

When the front door finally came open and I saw Charlie, I wished I'd been there sooner. He looked broken.

Fuck. Fuck me. His bottom lip trembled.

"Early this morning, Mary took her own life."

"Charlie—"

He shook his head. "She needs you."

"Where is she?"

"In her room with Manda."

Stepping in, I asked, "Why didn't anyone call me when... when you found out?"

"She wanted you safe, wanted your head in the Python matter. Didn't want to be a distraction."

"She never could be."

"I know, son. I know."

"Charlie, I'm so goddamn sorry."

He sucked in a shaky breath, then nodded. "Go to her, son."

Tagging the back of Charlie's neck, I gave it a squeeze. He nodded again. I let go and stalked down the hall to my woman's room. The door was already open. Poppy had curled into herself on the bed, facing the window. Manda was entwined around my woman, but her head came up and she looked over her shoulder. To me. After a nod, she bent in and whispered something to Poppy before coming off the bed.

Her hand landed on my arm. "She's awake," she said, and then walked out the door.

Reaching for the handle, I closed the door and quickly kicked off my boots and vest. "Baby?" I called. Nothing. "Poppy?" I said as I got to my knees to the bed. Shifting over, I took up Manda's position behind my woman. Only I stayed on one elbow and leaned over a little. Poppy was watching out the window.

There was no life in her eyes. She just looked and blinked.

Fuck.

Fucking hell.

She'd been crushed.

Slowly, I glided my hand up her arm, over her shoulder and then tucked her hair behind her ear. "Darlin'…. Jesus, Poppy, I'm so fuckin' sorry you lost her."

She closed her eyes. Only it didn't stop the tears leaking out.

"Baby, let me help. Let me take some of the pain, please."

Seeing her like this brought pressure to my chest and stabbing to my gut. It was killing me.

"Y-you can't."

"I can, darlin'."

"I want it," she whispered.

"Why?"

Suddenly, she spun around on the bed. Her head dug into my shoulder. I shot my arms around her body, holding her close.

"I-it's meant to hurt. I'm meant to feel it because she was such a wonderful, caring, amazing soul, and her leaving the earth i-is meant to be felt, even though i-it hurts so, so much."

"Then feel it, Poppy. Let it takeover you and let me be here for you when you need my strength."

She nodded into my neck. Her tears soaked my tee, but I didn't give a shit. Poppy was right. Mary was an amazing soul, and she left her mark on the world, so it was meant to be felt.

I wasn't sure how long I held her as she cried, as she felt the loss so deep it broke her apart, but eventually, she drifted off to sleep. I didn't move. I didn't give her words that were just that, words in a time when they weren't needed. I just held her through the night tightly to me, wishing I could take her pain, but knowing she was meant to have it.

It was early hours when her body jolted awake, her body tensing.

"Go back to sleep, darlin'. I got you."

"I-it wasn't a dream? A nightmare?"

"No, baby. Sorry."

She shifted, bringing her leg up over mine, twisting her arm more around my waist. "I need to see how Dad is." There wasn't a chance I'd tell her not to. Charlie would need her just as much as she needed the both of us. "But first, tell me some good news, my Miah. Did you get him?"

My Miah.

It was the first time she'd called me anything else other than Jerimiah.

My Miah.

She was claiming me.

I was hers.

"My Poppy." Her breath hitched. "We got him."

"It's over?"

"Yes, my Poppy, it's over."

And it was. But the way it happened… Christ. I never would've believed any of it could actually happen in real life, but it had.

Still, it didn't matter how it went down. It had, and it was over. Done forever.

Poppy didn't need to know all the details, and even when she was in the right frame of mind, I wasn't sure she should know everything. I'd make up my mind after talkin' to Charlie about it.

"How can I hurt so much and yet feel relieved? It doesn't make sense."

"Life never does."

"You do," she mumbled.

My lips twitched. "Sometimes."

She yawned, drained no doubt from feeling so much. "No. You do. When you said you thought I was your forever, you were right. I knew you were mine the day you saved me from tripping over."

My gut warmed. "Darlin', that was the first day you met me."

"I know." She nodded.

I smiled. "And I knew that day I caught you was the best thing that could have happened to me. Took me a little while to wake up, but when I did, I knew you were meant for me. Made to be my woman."

"Mum knew it too," she whispered. "She'd be happy you were here, in my life, in my heart, and becoming my forever."

My chest tightened.

She was damn right. Mary would have loved it, just as much as I did.

God, I hoped wherever she was, she was looking down at her girl and seeing I was taking care of her. Something I would do for the rest of my days.

CHAPTER EIGHTEEN

HOURS EARLIER

FANG

*a*fter leaving Blackie's, I called my woman, who I could still taste in my mouth, which I fuckin' loved, and told her I wasn't gonna get to her. Mentioned we'd had a lead, and that lead was taking me and my brothers to Python's mum's house.

Dodge, who I called after Poppy, to tell him what we had, was meeting us on the road about a block away from the house.

When we pulled around the corner, there would be

about twenty Harleys lining the streets, and the brothers were in a huddle at the front of the line. We pulled the four-by-four up the front, opposite Dodge, who was still astride his ride. Once seeing us, he climbed off and made his way over to the car, with his brothers following.

Soon as I had my door open, he asked, "You gonna be able to handle this?"

My head jerked back. "Are you?"

"Brother, it ain't my woman he's been fuckin' with. Know you wanna get your hands on him and do it in a way you can end his life, but we gotta question him. See if he's dealing with others we need to know about, to keep our territory clean."

My jaw clenched. "For the brotherhood, I'll keep my head."

His hand landed on my shoulder and applied pressure. "Just had to check, Fang. You get that?"

"Yeah." And I did. Any one of us were loose cannons when it came to the women in our lives. Still, I would keep it together long enough for the questioning to happen and then, *fuckin' then*, I'd have my time with him.

Dodge turned. "Right, let's get this motherfucker who attacked our club, messed with a brother's woman, and made our brothers bleed." He stalked through, the brothers parting along the way. Some took off, no doubt following their own orders, but I stuck with Dodge, Vicious, Dive, Gamer, and Muff. We made our way by foot so we didn't give our positions away, to get to the front of his ma's house.

"Lights are on," Dive commented.

"Strange, being this late," Gamer said. It was, since it was near morning. Something was up.

"Eyes peeled. The others are taking the sides and back of the house. Let's see if the fucker comes to the front door." Without a care, Dodge strolled through the gate first, with us following. He went right up to the door and rang the bell.

We heard noise within, then some clip-clop sound before the door was opened by an old lady leaning heavily on a walking cane.

"Hello." She smiled. "You must be who Blackie was talking about."

What. The. Ever-lovin'. Fuck.

She pushed the door open. "Come in, come in. Sorry, I'm not dressed for company, but when Blackie called, I was in bed." She'd obviously thrown a robe over herself and had then sat, waiting for our arrival.

I swore, if goddamn Blackie warned Python's ma, he was gonna have to deal with the consequences.

"Come sit," she ordered, and shuffled her way into a living room. I glanced around at my brothers' shocked faces.

"Are you coming?" she called.

Dodge came unstuck first and moved off the way she'd gone. The rest of us soon followed in a line behind.

When we entered, the woman was gesturing Dodge to sit on the couch. "Don't be shy, boys. Sit your butts down."

Dive and Vicious sat on each side of Dodge on the couch. Gamer, Muff, and I walked in to stand behind the couch, opposite the woman sitting in her own chair.

"You know why we're here?" Dodge asked.

She smiled. "Justice."

"What did Blackie tell you exactly?" I asked.

"Said I'd be gettin' a visit from the Hawks Motorcycle Club. Said you're after my Eric for what he's done to a girl. One who belongs to your club and Blackie's. And that Eric had shot up your place of business, harming two brothers."

"You seem pretty calm about this," Dive commented.

She snorted. "Been calm my whole life, boy. Knew I had to when my flesh and blood turned bad."

"Turned bad?" Vicious asked.

She eyed him, then shifted her gaze to all of us. "Hurts a mother when she loses love for her own son. But I couldn't love him no longer. Not after he took his daddy's life. At first I thought it was an accident, like he told me it was, but I see things, and I know Eric has dark growing in him. It's a dark not even a mother's love can heal. I tried." She nodded to herself. "I really tried."

"Do you get what's gonna happen to him when we get our hands on him?" Dodge asked.

"Yes." She stood, a bit shakily, but then straightened and goddamn asked, "Now, who wants a cup of coffee while we wait for him to get home?"

Holy motherfucking shit.

She was handing over her son to us, knowing we'd take his life.

"I'll take one." Dive smiled. "And I'll come help you."

"Oh, ain't you sweet." She waddled outta the room with Dive following, and the rest of us stayed stunned.

"Am I dreaming this?" Muff asked. "Not sure I'd want to dream of an old lady."

Gamer snorted. "She's handin' over her boy."

"Didn't you see?" Vicious asked.

"What?" Dodge replied.

"She's tired," he stated. "Done all she can for him, and she wants him to own up to his actions and face the consequences. In doing so, it brings justice."

I'D LOST count of the number of coffees we'd had. With a sad smile, Miriam, the fuckface's mum, ended up going to spend time at Blackie and Roda's, leaving us to wait for her son. My eyes were heavy as I sat in a kitchen chair, looking to the entryway of the living room with my gun on my thigh. Dive was asleep on the couch. Dodge paced the floor while Vicious stood leaning against a wall, and Gamer was in Miriam's vacant seat, resting. Muff lay on the floor with an arm thrown over his eyes. The only light in the room was spilling from the kitchen. It seemed Miriam, as she'd said, always left it on for Eric. The woman had even pulled the front curtain's closed so no one would see us before they entered. A peak of the sun shining filtered through the crack. I glanced to the clock to see that it was nearly mid-morning.

When in the hell was the cunt gonna show?

We knew he'd always come home, another thing Miriam had said. His arrival just depended on what was happening in his life.

When the lock turned in the door, I silently got to my feet and raised my gun. Dodge and Vicious moved to man each side of the living room entrance while Muff, Gamer, and Dive mimicked my move. We waited with our weapons trained.

"And then she sucked me dry. Best head I'd ever got."

My eyes shot wide, not because of the messed-up conversation we were hearing, but because I recognised that voice.

"That's all bitches are good for," another voice commented. Python.

"Damn right." The door shut, their footsteps pounding down the hall.

"Me ma should be up by now," Python said, a note of suspicion held in his voice.

"Ha. You still live with your momma."

"Shut the fuck up. The bitch knows her place even if she birthed me."

My face screwed up in disgust. A form entered the room, reached to the left and turned on the light. Then all hell broke loose.

Python tried to make a run for it, but Dodge reached out and punched him in the side of the face. Vicious took out his legs, and he fell to the floor while *Alvin* bent over a groaning Python on the floor and forced a knife right into his shoulder.

Yes. Fuckin' Alvin.

Poppy's brother.

Python screamed. He shoved at Alvin who stumbled back. With the knife embedded in his shoulder, Python got to his feet, backing himself into the corner of the room. He was outnumbered, he knew it. I could see the fear rise, but he pushed it back down when his eyes landed on me. His face changed, a sneer sliding across, and as he kept my gaze, he reached up and pulled the knife free from his shoulder.

"Was hopin' to see your face. Been watchin'. You visit my bitch the most. Know you want a taste of her."

I smirked. "Don't want. Got. She's mine."

"Won't be for long. I'll take her, make her mine again, just like I've had her."

Muff snorted. "You're seriously not too bright. You're outnumbered, dickhead."

I saw it. The way he flinched, as if he were about to move. He was gonna use that knife he held. His eyes hadn't left me, even as Muff spoke. I knew I would be his target. Though, I wasn't the only one who saw it.

As Python lifted the knife and threw it my way, Gamer came at me, taking me to the ground. Muff fired off a shot, but it was Alvin who pulled another knife from somewhere and hurled it at Python, slicing his blade straight into his throat. Alvin followed the knife, gripped it and held it there. They both went to the ground, to their knees, and then Alvin laid Python to the floor. The life in Python's eyes leaked out as he weakly gripped Alvin's wrists.

Alvin spoke. "I messed up. Fucked my family over. Gotta make it right before I disappear. Heard what's been going down, and you had to die by my hand. Want you to know my sister will live on, and she'll be doin' it happy. She'll do it with a guy she's loved her whole life. You'll be nothing to her. You've always been *nothing* to her."

Fuck me.

Python gurgled something out as his back hit the ground. Alvin smiled and shook his head. "You fool.

She'll never remember you because she'll be too happy to remember."

Silence.

Nothing but air.

Alvin straightened, letting go of the knife. He turned to Dodge as Gamer and I got to our feet. "Didn't expect you lot here." He grinned.

"We had plans for that motherfucker, kid," Dodge barked.

Alvin shrugged. "So did I."

"He made our club bleed."

"He tormented *my* sister," Alvin fired back.

Muff scoffed. "So did you."

Alvin rolled his eyes. "I'm her brother. I had the right to."

"Just what in the fuck are you doin' here, Alvin, and why?" I demanded.

His jaw clenched, seriousness taking over his expression. "Redemption."

My body locked.

"I've made a lot of mistakes. Needed to save myself and make up for things before I head out."

"Head out?" Vicious asked.

"Gonna disappear for a while." His eyes hit mine. "She asked me to help her."

"Who?"

Fuck me. His eyes suddenly filled with tears.

"Been to see her since gettin' out. She wanted my help, *begged* for it. I gave it, but I can't face them after it." His bottom lip trembled. Christ, what had he done? "Poppy's safe. She'll be happy... eventually. After this pain passes, she'll be the happiest she's ever been. You'll make sure of it, I know. And, with time, Dad will be as well."

"Alvin, what are you talking about?"

He shook his head. "She *begged me*. It was the least I could do for her, give her, since I'd given her nothing before but heartache. It killed me. Cut me so deep, but I helped her." His eyes closed, his hands fisting.

"Alvin?" I pressed.

His grief-filled eyes came up to meet mine. "Poppy'll need you right now. You have to go to her."

"Why?"

"Because I helped Mum end her life."

CHAPTER NINETEEN

POPPY

I stood up the front with my dad on one side, my hand in his, and Jerimiah on the other, his arm around my waist. The funeral minister had just said his final words, and they were lowing Mum's coffin into the ground.

Lowering her into her final resting place.

She was gone.

My mum was gone.

The sun was shining down on us as we listened to her final song. I couldn't understand how the day could be bright and warm, when it should have been weeping like I was. It should have been cloudy and dull, like I felt.

My brother hadn't shown, but I didn't expect him to.

It was only days ago I found out he had a hand in helping Mum get the medicine she needed to overdose. I understood why Jerimiah had been reluctant to tell me, since when Charlie and Jerimiah had sat me down, I'd lost it. I'd wanted to find Alvin and kill him. I even tried to get out of the house to seek him out. Jerimiah and Dad eventually calmed me down enough to make me understand. Jerimiah had explained how Alvin, even though it had wrecked him, did what Mum asked because he hated the pain she lived in knowing she was hurting us. Only it wasn't her hurting us. It was her disease.

At first, it was hard to understand her reasoning, but then I had to put myself in her position. I wouldn't want my family to go through the anguish we felt when Mum had been lost in her mind to us. What also helped was when I read her note the night before her funeral.

I'd been putting it off, knowing it was going to hurt reading it, seeing her words.

Jerimiah, who hadn't left my side since I'd found out about Mum, sat beside me on my bed when I pulled the letter from my drawer and said it was time. Actually, I wasn't just sitting beside Jerimiah; he commandeered my body by lifting me up and planting my butt between his spread legs. His arms wound around, one at my lower stomach and one at my chest.

With his kiss to my temple, I opened the letter.

To my beautiful star,

I'm so sorry I've hurt you over this, Poppy. I know by now you've heard I took my life. I need you to grasp why I would do such a thing. On my good days, when you and your father visited, I saw the despair in each of your eyes until you knew I was myself, and then your love shone through.

When I found my own notes to myself, I knew I was putting my family through hell. It's the despair I can't bear seeing. I struggle with how my illness brings such pain to the people I love, and even though you're hurting from it, I know my family, each and every one of you, visit me each and every day because of the love we share for one another.

This is my last chance to give something to my family, to you, before I lose myself completely.

I love you, my star. Forever and ever.

I know you will have a beautiful life with Jerimiah. He's an amazing soul for my daughter. One who will guide you, protect you, and love you with every breath he takes. Hold tight to him and love him back just as much.

I know it will be hard, but please forgive your brother one day. He's given me what I want, and it was after some begging and crying on my part. He was lost. We didn't realise just how lost he was because... some things have happened to him. I won't say what. It's his story, and don't go searching through my things. I've burned that note to myself. But he's finally found himself, and one day, I hope my family will be together again.

You, my beautiful, stubborn, wonderful girl, need to live your life to the fullest. Cherish each day, my star. I'll be watching from above, and I'll be doing it smiling because I'm already proud of the woman you've become.

I give you so much love, always.

Mum xx

Just remembering her note brought fresh tears to my eyes. I let them fall. I wouldn't hold them back. I'd accepted that feeling her loss was meant to hurt.

"We therefore commit her body to the ground: earth to earth, ashes to ashes, dust to dust; in the sure and certain hope of the Resurrection to eternal life," the minister finished.

Dropping my hand, Dad stepped forward, picked up some dirt and sprinkled it over Mum's lowered coffin. Once he was back beside me, I took my turn.

I watched the dirt leave my hand, scattering to the wood below. "I'll miss you, Mum."

THE REST of the day was a daze. Blackie and Roda put together the post-funeral reception at the Venom MC compound in their common area. It was big enough for everyone to attend. I hadn't realised how many would be there. I didn't take notice until at the end of the funeral, when I turned and found not only the Venom MC at my back, but the Hawks as well.

"Honey, you should eat something," Dad suggested.

I gave him a sad smile. "So should you, Dad."

"Both of you should," Roda put in, appearing from behind us while Dad and I sat at one of the tables. "So here." She placed two plates down, piled with all types of food. I met Jerimiah's stare from across the room, where he stood talking with Blackie, and rolled my eyes. He grinned back.

"He's smitten," Roda commented, pulling up a chair.

"Just as much as I am with him. I only wish…."

Roda reached over and placed her hand on mine. I pulled my gaze up from the table to hers. "Baby girl, your momma would be lookin' down upon you and be ecstatic with the way you two are with each other."

"Roda's right," Dad said. "The way he keeps track of you would have your ma gushing over it. Proud to have him in the family."

"We're not talking marriage or anything yet."

Roda laughed. "You said *yet*."

Dad grinned, then sobered. His jaw clenched, his

nostrils flared. "We'll miss your mum forever and a day, Poppy. But she'd be happy for you, just like I am with havin' Fang at your side. He's a good person. Just the right man for my girl."

"Dad," I whispered, my eyes filling with tears.

"Am I interrupting something?" Leanna, Jerimiah's mum, asked, standing at the side of the table.

Dad cleared his throat. "No, please sit."

"We were just talking about your son," Roda supplied.

"Roda." I gasped.

"Pfft. Lee-lee knows how good of a boy she's got."

Leanna smiled. "I do. I also know how good of a woman he's picked for himself."

"Leanna—"

"Pish-posh." She waved her hand. "I'm happy for you both, and glad he can be there for you right now. I just wish…."

Dad surprised me by taking her hand. "Mary knows." He shook his head. "She knew how much you cared for her. The letters helped her understand everything."

Letters?

After things went down with everyone finding out about Switch and his preference for teens, Leanna distanced herself from the club, even her friends, but Mum had always spoken of Leanna fondly, so I presumed they were still in contact in some way. I just didn't know it was through letters. Then again, I should have guessed.

Mum did love to write; it had always been a hobby of hers.

My body jolted when Blackie spoke up with a loud, demanding voice. "I'd like to toast to Mary Torian. A beautiful soul, a wonderful woman, and she will be missed by many."

"To Mary," Jerimiah added, his own voice reached out to all.

Drinks were raised, my own included. I smiled sadly at Dad, and he returned it. And as I sat there surrounded by people who cared, who I classed as family and friends, I realised Mum would have loved the day. She always enjoyed family days at the compound.

Glancing back over at Jerimiah, who was already looking my way, I thought... no matter where I was, whether it was here at the Venom compound or even at the Hawks compound, as long as I had him with me, it didn't matter whose family we were surrounded by.

As long as I had him.

CHAPTER TWENTY

FANG

A few weeks later, when Poppy said she wanted to do something, I suggested a night at Pick's bar. After all, it was the place we'd had our first kiss, and I was hoping to re-enact it. I wasn't some sleaze gunning for a piece of my woman's arse while she was grieving, but it was getting harder and harder to resist starting something since I slept next to her each night. Holding her in my arms, kissing her cheek, her temple, her neck, and a brief peck on her lips. Waking up finding her booty snuggling against my morning wood was like torture.

Still, there was no way I would force something from her. She wasn't ready. I'd wait until I knew for sure, until she made the first move and showed me she wanted me for more than comfort. Not that I was complaining. I loved being there for her.

At first, I'd been worried when I suggested Pick and Billy's pub, since it was also the place she saw Python. However, she'd put my mind at ease with a smile, and she'd said, "I like that idea. A night to spend with friends, my man, and booze under one roof."

She'd meant her new Hawks friends too. Nary, Low, Mena, Lissa, Della, and Josie had taken not only Poppy, but Manda under their wings. Brought them into the pussy posse fold. It had happened a few days after Mary's funeral when they'd arrived at Poppy's place and kicked Charlie and me out by stating Poppy needed her girl time.

Wasn't sure what they talked about or what they did, but hours later when Poppy had texted it was safe to come back, I did, and it was to a relaxed, happier Poppy. She was getting back to herself. Still, knew there'd be moments her mum's death would be fresh in her heart and mind. Then I'd be there for her.

"Where are your thoughts at?" my woman asked after she rejoined me in the booth we'd occupied with some brothers and their old ladies.

"Thinkin' about you." I grinned. Dive stood so she could scoot close to my side. I wrapped my arm around her shoulders and touched my mouth to just below her ear. She sighed happily.

"I hope it was good thoughts."

"They always are." I told her the truth.

"Good." She smiled, and then, for the first time, she leaned into me and—

"Yo, Fang. Your turn for a round of beers," Muff called.

Fuckin' shit.

I'd just about had my woman's mouth, with *her* kissing *me,* and the dick interrupted. By the smirk on his smug face, he knew it too. Manda, who was curled into his side, giggled.

"Actually, it's Kalen's turn," Mena said. She took her man's hand and pulled him from the booth. She may have thought I didn't see it, but I caught the smile she sent Poppy.

"Come on, handsome. It's time to get our groove on." Manda winked at Poppy before she took Muff's hand and led him out to the dance floor. He was happy to follow. My brother was into Manda in a big way. Poppy confirmed it just the other day that Manda was over-the-moon taken by Muff. It was good to see.

Turning back to Poppy, I raised my brows, grinning. "I get the feelin' your girls were helping you clear the booth for some reason."

Her lips twitched. "I don't know what you're talking about."

Tucking her hair behind her ear, I asked, "Just what was said in that bathroom trip?"

"Hmm, a lot of things."

My goddamn body jolted when her hand landed on my thigh and rubbed up and down.

Glancing down, I watched her hand for a moment and then looked back up to find my woman smirking.

"What *type* of things exactly?" I questioned. I had to be sure it wasn't my dick making my mind jump to conclusions. Because right then, it was singing, *"Our woman wants a piece of us."*

"Let's see. Manda said I should just jump you right here and now. While Mena suggested a more subtle approach, by saying I should just ask to see your room at the compound."

I shouldn't have taken a sip of beer when she spoke. My throat closed over. The beer stuck, and I choked on what was left in my mouth. Brothers around the booth started laughing, while Poppy patted me on my back.

Clearing my throat, I said, "You… you wanna see my room?"

Her leg came over mine. She scooted her butt closer and wound her arms around my neck. "Yes, Jerimiah. I want to see your room because I'm ready. You've been my rock through everything. My one and only, and I love that you've wanted to take care of me. But having you in my bed for the past three weeks without you making a move on me has been torture."

I jerked my head back, surprised. "You've wanted me to make a move on you?"

"If rubbing my butt against you each morning wasn't enough, then you should have guessed each time I'd tried to take a kiss deeper."

"I didn't want to push you... with, you, ah, your mum...."

She giggled. Where in the fuck had my man balls gone? Though, I was on the verge of throwing her over my shoulder and running from the room to get back to the compound.

"Yes, I've been grieving, but I'm still a woman."

"My woman," I growled in the back of my throat.

"Yes." She nodded, smiling.

Cupping the side of her face, I used my other hand to slide through her hair and stopped at the back of her head where I gently pulled her forward so our lips just touched. There, while keeping her warmed gaze, I said, "So if my woman wants her man, I won't say no. But I do want you to know I fuckin' love you."

Tears swam in her eyes. "Love you, my Miah."

Closing my eyes, I just felt it. Felt her words. And it was something goddamn amazing the way her words heated me all over. Groaning against her lips, I pushed my mouth against hers. She moaned in response, her mouth parting enough for me to guide my tongue to just past her lips. Poppy opened her mouth wider, her hands gripping my cut and tugging me closer still. Our tongues touched, tasted, and then danced against one another.

My heart beat in ecstasy. I shifted my hand from her cheek down her shoulder, arm, and then under, to her waist, holding tight.

Catcalls and wolf whistles surrounded us, and reluctantly, I pulled back, but not before another quick peck, quick taste, of my woman.

A throat cleared behind me, from the booth next to ours. "If I didn't like Beast's cock so much, that kiss would'a turned me on."

Poppy laughed, burying her head in the crook of my neck and shoulder. Looking over my shoulder, I glared, but it wasn't a full one.

"In fact, I'm sure a lot of the brothers will leave soon wanting a piece from their woman… or man." Knife glanced at a grinning Beast. "Babe, I'm ready to go. You?"

"Sure." He winked.

"Shut the fuck up," I clipped.

Everyone laughed.

Dipping my head, I whispered into Poppy's ear, over her laughter, "Wanna get outta here?"

She pulled back, ran her hand up my chest and bit her

bottom lip. But it was her nod that had my cock hardening.

Of course the brothers couldn't leave it at that. As we got out of the booth and started for the door, a lot of them were clapping, and encouraging, "Go claim your woman, Fang."

Fuck me.

"Stupid dicks," I muttered when we hit outside.

Poppy curled both hands around my arm. "They're just having some fun."

"At our expense."

"Doesn't bother me. As long as I know you won't back out."

I stopped. Poppy's body jolted back since she'd still been moving. "You think I'd back out?"

"Well, I hope not, but you might think it's too soon." She shifted to stand in front of me. "I promise you, Jerimiah, I'm okay. Over everything. Yes, it's hard to know she's gone. So hard some days I can't breathe, but then all I have to do is think of you, and the oxygen rushes in, because I know that what we have is something special. It's a future I want. A future I look forward to."

"A future I'd dreamed of for so bloody long," I admit. "I'm just sorry we both got lost along the way."

"So am I. Although, now I'm very *not* sorry because I'm right where I want to be."

"Where?"

"In your life, in your arms, and soon to be in your bed."

"Fuck," I bit out. "Let's get out of here."

"Yes, please."

POPPY

Thank God the pub wasn't far from the compound. My body was heating, my clit tingling, my nipples hard, and each hot glance Jerimiah directed my way made me worse.

"I'm sorry I don't have the.... It's a room at the compound." His jaw clenched. The discomfort he showed about the place was sweet. It made the night so much more because it showed he cared. He wanted things perfect, special. Didn't he understand they already were because I had him next to me?

And soon in me. *Yay.*

Jesus, I had to rub my legs together. Shaking my head, I said, "It doesn't matter where, as long as you're there, and you want this."

"Are you crazy, woman?" He snorted, then muttered to himself as he opened his door, "If I want his." Another snort. He was at my side of the car before I had my door opened, and then he was pointing down at his erection behind his jeans. In an annoyed, and slightly pissed off tone, he clipped, "I've been walking around hard most of the time since I saw you in that towel. Of fuckin' course I want this. You're mine. For-fuckin'-ever."

Grinning up at him like a mad woman, I replied, "Then take me to bed, Hulk."

His control slipped, his eyes darkening, making me gasp and my clit tingle again. Reaching in, Jerimiah undid my seat belt, picked me up, and next I was over his shoulder while he strode to the entrance of the compound.

Laughing, I swatted his sexy butt, causing him to grunt. A door opened, and as he walked us past the door, I watched it close.

"Hoo-boy, someone's finally gettin' herself some," Low bellowed.

"Little bird," Dodge bit out.

She ignored him. "Go get him, girl."

"I think it's the other way around, Low. He's gonna go get himself some."

I pushed up from Jerimiah's back, as he disregarded everything going on around us and kept walking, to see a hot guy in jeans and a... pink tee. "Though, I wouldn't mind givin' him some," he added, which caused the guy next to him to snap, "Julian."

"What? Not that I would. You're man enough for me, poppet." Before the next door closed, I caught Julian's gaze. He gave me the thumbs-up. Laughter once again bubbled up and out of me.

It'd been a while since I felt so much happiness inside of me.

It felt strange and confusing. It had me wondering if I should feel guilty for having these emotions since I'd lost my mum.

Then again, she'd wanted Dad and me to go on and live our lives to the fullest... and I was going to.

CHAPTER TWENTY-ONE

POPPY

*I*nside Jerimiah's bedroom, he placed me on my feet and then closed the door. Glancing around, I noticed how tidy things were. The bed was made. There were no clothes scattering the floor; instead, I saw a basket in the corner with his dirty pile in it. Even his desk in the other corner of the room was tidy.

"You're a clean freak," I said, standing in the middle of the room. I turned back to my man, who stood near the door leaning against it. I smiled. "At least when we move in together, I won't have to do all the cleaning."

His eyes darkened even more. "We're moving in together?"

My mouth dropped open. I closed it and then opened it to say, "Well, eventually. But not for a while. I have to stay with Dad, and you can... ah, you know, continue staying there with us... for a while."

He smirked. "You're never getting rid of me now, darlin'. Especially after tonight. Once I have all of you in every way,"—my clit pulsed— "there'll be no escaping me."

"I wouldn't want to."

"Good." He straightened, and *poof*, there went his tee to the floor. "Saw some pills in the bathroom at your place one morning."

I nodded, my gaze running over Jerimiah's body. I'd seen it a million times, but still, it would never be enough. Each time was like a treasure. "Birth control."

He grunted, and I watched his hands undo the top button of his jeans... then I waited, but he didn't do anything else. *Strip damn it,* I wanted to yell. Moving my gaze up slowly, I met his. He cleared his throat. "Are you a virgin?"

My stomach clenched. Would he feel differently for me when I told him I wasn't? There'd been one night when I was living with my aunt and had gone out with some friends where I drank too much and just wanted to forget.

"I understand," he muttered, then bit his bottom lip

before running a hand over his face, clenching both hands down at his sides. He knew, without even me saying it. We knew each other too well sometimes. "I hate it, but I get it. And I'm no saint."

I snorted. No, he definitely wasn't. "The past is the past. We look to the future."

"Our future," he stated roughly.

"Yes," I whispered.

"Come here," he ordered gruffly. Any other time I would have snapped something back about ordering me around, but *I* wanted to be beside him. In his arms.

I stopped just in front of him. His eyes travelled over my body, from the top of my head right down to my toes. Tipping my head back, I caught his gaze as his hands landed on my hips.

"So short." He smirked. I glared. "Perfect size for me."

"Hell yes I am."

"Wanted you for such a goddamn long time."

"Now you have me."

"I do." His fingers tickled under my tee. "Been waiting to see you naked for a long time too." He smiled. "Used to peek, back in the day, whenever you got changed for bed."

I laughed. "Did you now?"

"Shit yes." He leaned down. His mouth touched mine, but only for a moment. "One time, when it was early in the morning, I woke to you lying next to me, but your tee had ridden up."

God, his voice was so low and enticing. I licked my lips, and since we were so close, my tongue touched his lips. He groaned. I asked, "W-what did you do?"

"I wanted to lick them, suck on them, and play with them. But I didn't." His hands slid up further, cupping both breasts. I gasped, and my clit pulsed. "I did do something though."

"What?" I whispered.

He didn't answer right away. Instead, he released his hold and pulled my tee over my head, dropping it to the floor.

"Fuck," he clipped, eyeing my black-laced chest. Reaching around, I unclasped my bra and pulled it from my body, throwing it to the floor. "So goddamn beautiful." His hands once again came up and cupped each breast.

"What did you do, my Miah?"

He chuckled low. Holy hell, was that a blush coating his cheeks? Yes, yes it was. Bending, he kissed each mound before lifting to capture my lips. Against them, after a burning, deep kiss, he mumbled, "I jerked off, looking at them."

Oh God.

I wished I'd had known. I would have loved to have seen it.

"Never come so hard before. Just the sight of your tits had me crazy."

"You should have woken me."

"What would you have done?"

His head rocked back when I palmed his hardness behind his jeans and ran my hand up and down it. "I would have helped."

"Shit," he bit out. "Fuck," he snarled. His head descended and he pressed his lips to mine, and kissed me hard, wet, and long. His hands ran over my upper body, like mine were doing to him.

Always. I'd always wanted to touch him this way. His back, his sides, his powerful arms and... hell yes, his hard, muscled stomach. Over the ridges, into the valleys of his six-pack. Playfully, I pinched each nipple. He chuckled against my mouth, only to return the favour. I whimpered against his lips. His hands tightened on me. One then glided down to grab my butt, the other moving to the front of my jeans.

His lips left mine, and I panted while he kissed down my neck, to my shoulder, chest, and then he sucked a nipple into his mouth. "Miah," I moaned.

Somehow without my knowing, my jeans were undone, and his fingers teased the top of my skin. "Please," I begged. I needed him to touch me.

"You want me to play with you, darlin'?" he asked against my neck.

"Yes."

When his hand dipped in, I closed my eyes and bit my bottom lip. "Spread," he ordered. I did. Even though my legs were weak, I parted them more and was rewarded with his fingers sliding through my wetness and straight inside of me. "Fuck."

"Yes," I cried, thrusting my hips forward and down to take his fingers deeper.

His free hand gripped my hair and tugged my head back. He straightened, and our heated eyes caught. "Fuck yourself on my fingers, Poppy."

Panting, I nodded. Riding up and down on his fingers, I groaned in pleasure when the edge of his palm rubbed my clit.

"M-Miah," I stuttered, lost, close already.

"Yeah, baby. Fuck yourself and come for me," he demanded roughly against my neck, where his teeth sank in next.

I cried out from the pleasure and pain. Still riding his fingers, I gripped his shoulders hard to hold myself up, only to nearly stumble back when he released my hair and slid his hand out of my pants. "Jeans off, darlin'. Lie on the bed and spread wide for your man. Want to watch your pussy come over my fingers."

Please. Yes, please. Nodding, I stepped back again and hooked my thumbs into my jeans at my hips, ready to whip them off. Then I paused.

I paused.

And I did it because I was too busy eating Jerimiah up with my eyes as he undid his jeans, slipped his hand in and pulled his impressive cock free, before he ran his hand up and down.

"Poppy."

"Hmm?"

He chuckled.

"Jesus, darlin', try to drag your eyes from my cock and get your sweet arse on that bed." Another laugh. "Didn't realise my cock would put you in a trance, baby."

I snapped, "You put it away."

He snorted. "Yeah, because your man wants his fingers inside you, and the way you're looking at my dick, you'll see him coming too soon. I ain't wasting it over my hand when it can be in you."

"O-okay." I couldn't argue with that. Kicking off my shoes, I slipped my jeans down my legs, along with my panties, and flung them to the side with my foot.

"Stunning," Jerimiah growled, and even before I managed to lie on the bed, I was swooped up into his arms. His mouth claimed mine. Our tongues tasted and played as he walked us to the bed. He bent, flattening my back to the mattress.

Jerimiah kissed his way down over my neck, chest, and stomach, where I bit back a laugh because it tickled. Down lower, he kissed my mound and with his hand on my inner thighs, he parted my legs. "Sexy as fuck," he clipped. Dipping in, he touched his mouth to my clit, slid his tongue down and slipped it inside of me. I moaned, arching my back, tangling my hands in the bed covers.

"Miah," I whispered. He pulled back, his hot, smouldering eyes meeting mine. Then he inserted two fingers.

"You gonna come on my fingers, baby?" he asked with a roughness in his sultry voice.

I nodded, my hands tightening even more. He glided in and out of me, watching what he was doing to me. "So wet, so tight. All mine to enjoy."

"Yes, handsome," I murmured. "God," I cried as my belly dipped, and tightened.

"Eyes on me, Poppy," he ordered. I looked down. He glanced up to make sure I was watching before his full attention went back to his hand driving in and out of me. Driving *me* crazy. "Ground down," he clipped, his fingers deep once again.

I did.

I ground down and lost myself.

My walls clenched around his fingers. His eyes darkened more, eyeing my pussy coming over his fingers. "Beautiful." He slipped his fingers free, pulling them up to suck them clean. "Fuck, Poppy, you taste better than I thought you would, and I've thought about it a lot."

Smiling sedately up at him, I slowly sat. "Now is it my

turn to taste you." When I reached for his jeans, his erection evident behind them, he grabbed my wrists.

"Another time, darlin'. I'm leakin' already for you. Need inside your sweet pussy."

"Just one lick?"

He chuckled. "Next time. Wanna spill inside you for the first time, not in your mouth." Stepping back, he dragged his jeans down his thick thighs and kicked them off to the side. When he lost his boots and socks, I didn't know.

"How do you want me?" Licking my lips, I watched him stroke himself.

"On your knees, baby. Hands to the headboard."

Nodding, I slipped to my hands and knees, and knee walked up the bed. The mattress compressed behind with his weight joining me. I gripped the headboard as he instructed, glancing over my shoulder.

"Jut your arse out for me." I did. "Christ," he growled. "Fuckin' love your body."

"As I love yours."

His hands landed on my hips, ran up my sides, and then back down over my arse. They circled, gripped and smacked down on my skin. "Miah," I cried. My head dropped forward, chin to my chest as I lost myself to the sensation of my man touching my body everywhere he could. Running his hands up once again and around to my breasts, he then clutched them, sweeping his fingers over my tender nipples.

Jerimiah shifted forward, rubbing his erection against my arse. I pushed back to hear him suck in a breath. A hand tugged my hair, and my head dropped back. His lips touched my neck, opened, and then he sunk his teeth into my skin.

His other hand moved between us, gripping himself. "Arse up," he ordered, licking the spot he'd bitten. Sticking my arse out and up, I felt his fingers toying with my entrance and then it was the head of his cock.

"Ready for me, my Poppy?"

"Always, my Miah."

Slowly, he guided himself inside of me. So very slowly. His hand in my hair loosened and then disappeared to come around the front of me, to my belly, rubbing, then sliding up to cup my breast.

"Best feeling ever, sinking into my woman."

Looking over my shoulder, I moaned when he filled me completely. My lips parted in a pant. He pulled back, and then thrust back in, causing me to cry out his name.

"Gotta fuck you, baby."

"Yes."

Both hands went back to my hips. I tightened my hold on the headboard before he picked up his pace, drilling his cock into me over and over.

His arms wrapped me up. One around my lower belly, the other across my chest, still fucking me deliciously.

My body tensed, my belly dipped once again, and that pleasurable tightening started. "I-I'm... coming!" I yelled. My pussy tightened around his cock, which still slid in and out of me fast.

"Fuck," he snarled. "Christ," he groaned. "Love you," he grunted, before I felt him swell, planting himself deep and coming apart.

Slipping from within me, he moved back a little and picked me up. I let out a surprised squeal, then laughed when he deposited me on the bed. He moved the covers and climbed in beside me, wrapping me up in a nice Jerimiah package again. Both arms cradled me, one behind my neck, the other over my waist, and one leg over both of mine.

"You good with me in you?"

I giggled. "As long as you don't mind a wet patch."

"Don't give a shit."

"Are we sleeping?"

"Darlin', I just came harder than the time I did looking at your tits. Need a nap, and then a second round, followed by a third. Then maybe I'll feed you so we can go again."

Hmm, yes please.

"The way you snuggled into me, guess you like that plan."

"Yes, handsome. I like that plan very much."

"Good."

"Love you, Miah."

His reply was to kiss me soundly, and I didn't mind that at all.

CHAPTER TWENTY-TWO

FANG

"I'll see you soon then?" I asked Poppy on the phone. I'd arrived early at my mum's to help her set up for lunch. Poppy was supposed to come with me, but she'd run to Beast and Knife's to watch Nevaeh. Beast was already working and Knife had to head out to do a few things, not wanting to take Nevaeh with him since she had a fever and the day was a cold, wet one.

"Yes, Knife's on his way back, and then I want to pick up some cakes to bring for dessert."

"Darlin', Mum's got a shitload already. You don't need to bring anything."

"Miah, it's cakes, no one can never have enough."

"Christ, all right, but you know we'll just end up takin' them home."

"Again, it's cakes. Would that really bother you, Dad, or me...? Don't bother, I know the answers a big fat no. See you soon."

She was right. I grunted. "Love you."

"Love you back," she said softly into the phone, and then hung up. I'd never get tired of hearing her say that. Each time was like a shot of goddamn bliss to the heart.

"Aw, look at that. Even after three months, he's still got it bad for her," Roda said, appearing out of nowhere.

"Sometimes I have to go to bed early just to get away from the mush," Charlie teased with a smile, and then took a swig of his beer.

"I think it's beautiful," Mum bragged, before swatting Charlie in the back of the head. They'd become close over the last few months. Only friendship, but it was good to see. They both needed it.

"Where in the hell is everyone when a brother needs help with all this shit?" was yelled from the front of the house.

Roda scoffed. "It's not that much. Just get your black arse in here with it."

Blackie strode in with his arms chock-full of trays, boxes, and bowls.

"Roda, I told you I had the food handled," Ma complained.

"Woman, I told you I can't come to a lunch without bringing anything."

Blackie grumbled about something as he laid shit out while I sent off a quick text to Poppy, stating Roda had arrived armed with a mountain of food. Her reply was instant.

Poppy: :P I'm still going to get cakes. I'll have the girls over and we'll finish off what we don't eat today.

"Poppy's going to organise a girls' night to finish off all the food," I said, more to Charlie than anyone since we were still living under his roof.

"Fuck," he clipped.

Fuck was right. When the women got together, you never knew what was gonna go down. The last time it was at Charlie's, I took him out to the pub for a while, and when we got back, it was to find Julian stripping on the living room coffee table while the women screamed crazily at him. Lucky the guy was gay, or shit would have hit the fan.

"Oooh, that sounds like a good night." Roda clapped. Charlie, Blackie, and I looked at each other.

Our clubs helped one another out from time to time, but things were changing for the better. Blackie and Roda were invited to family days at the Hawks compound, since they were in mine and Poppy's life, and with Charlie being a Venom, it was bound to happen.

Soon, if not already, the women would conspire to

just join the clubs together in some way. Roda loved the Hawks pussy posse. Only, it'd never happen unless Blackie stopped dealing in flesh. And knowing Blackie, he wouldn't; he liked the money the girls brought in.

"Roda—" Blackie started. He stepped close to his woman, ready to give her a piece of his mind.

Her hand came up in his face. "Don't you Roda me in that tone. They're my girls, no matter where they come from. I ain't asking we switch patches. We're Venom. Doesn't mean we can't have friends. Hell, they're so far in my heart I'd cut anyone who fucked with any of them." Her eyes narrowed. "And I'd cut a brother if they tried to take my girls from me."

Blackie glared back, snorted, and then leaned in to kiss her. "Glad we got that sorted."

Roda laughed. "Me too, baby." She swatted his arse when he turned back to the food. "Means you'll be gettin' some tonight," she sang.

I cringed. Charlie groaned as if he was in pain from hearing that, and Mum giggled.

Only it all fell silent in the next second.

It all fell silent when we heard a bang out the back.

My phone picked that moment to ring. Charlie and Blackie started for the back door while I answered a call from Parker. "Brother?"

"Shit. Fuck, Fang. I didn't know until now."

"What?" I barked. Mum froze, Roda went right to her, curling her arm around her shoulders.

"Been searchin', brother. Got nothin' until just now."

Christ. Switch.

"Where?"

A shot was fired outside. I took off towards the hall to the back door, only to come to an abrupt halt when the back door opened, and Charlie was pushed in.

"Fang? What the fuck was that?"

"Don't matter, brother," I said into the phone.

"He's there?" Parker asked in a quiet, deadly tone.

"Get off the phone," Switch snarled. Shoving Charlie again, he stumbled, but caught his hands on the wall to steady himself. It was then I saw Switch had a gun pointed on Charlie.

If anything happened to Poppy's dad....

"Fuck," Parker said before I ended the call.

"Throw it to the ground," Switch ordered. "And back up."

I did.

I kept backing until I was in front of Mum and Roda hugging each other. Charlie entered, Switch behind him.

"Perfect day for a family reunion." Switch laughed.

"Where's my man?" Roda asked.

Switch met her gaze and chuckled again.

"Where's my man?" Roda screamed.

"Bleeding out hopefully," Switch answered.

Roda made a move to go around me, but I put my arm out to stop her. "No," she cried. "No!" she shouted, and then pounded my back.

"He'll be okay," Charlie comforted, and got a hit to the back of the head for it. Mum gasped.

Roda yelled, "I'm gonna kill you."

"Ma," I called.

"Roda, come on," Mum said quietly. Then I heard her whisper something to Roda, and I lost her weight from my back.

"Leanna, good to see you, lovely."

"Fuck off, Switch."

Switch snorted. "That any way to talk to your man."

"What do you want?" I demanded, before Mum said anything. Switch just wanted to play mind games with her, with us all, but I wouldn't fuckin' have it.

"Ah, my son. Heard you were looking for me, so I thought I'd pay you a visit and clean up a few messes before I head out of Australia for good."

He was one fuckin' idiot if he thought he was leaving.

"I see that look, son. Know you were on the phone to your pig. Know he'll be on his way. So I'll make things quick." He pulled his gun from Charlie and aimed it at me.

"Don't," Mum screamed.

Switch sneered. "You'll be following him. You all will."

"No, they won't."

No. Fuck me, no, no, no.

"Poppy, get outta here," I bit out.

Switch's eyes widened. "Poppy? The piece I tried to get to heel but Blackie interrupted that night."

My jaw clenched. My heart was fuckin' going crazy while my body trembled in fury.

"I'm not going anywhere," Poppy said from behind Switch.

Switch didn't have a care in the world with Poppy at his back. He'd think she was weak, but I knew my woman.

"You think you can threaten the people I love?" Poppy demanded, her voice high with emotion. Probably fear and anger.

"Just fuck off, sweetheart. I'll deal with you later."

"You'll not harm anyone, motherfucker."

A gun was fired. Switch cried out, and I dove for Roda and Mum, while Charlie spun around and smashed his fist into Switch's face. Switch hit the floor and tried to get up straight away, until Poppy hovered over his head, a gun in her hand, and aimed it between his eyes.

I scrambled to my feet, back over to the doorway. "Poppy," I called softly. Blood dripped from Switch, making a pool of red under his left leg.

"He was going to hurt you all," she whispered.

"Honey, we're fine. Put the gun down," Charlie tried.

"He was going to shoot you all," Poppy shouted. "I would have lost you all."

Fuck. Fuck. Fuck. Her bottom lip trembled.

"Darlin', you wouldn't have," I said.

"H-how do you know?"

"Because I would have gone Hulk on him eventually."

She snorted, wiped at her eyes, but didn't move the gun away from him. Switch was smart enough to keep his trap shut. She'd already made him bleed. He finally understood she was capable of doing it again.

She shook her head. "I won't risk any of you. He's already hurt Blackie."

Christ, what could I say to get her to back off? I didn't want her to take a life. I didn't want that mark upon her soul when mine was already dark. I had to protect her from making the choice of taking a life, even when Switch's needed to end.

Mum came up beside me. "Poppy, please, baby girl, don't." At first, I thought she was going to defend Switch, but then she added, "He needs to rot in jail like the piece of rubbish he is. Let him live his life in hell."

"Poppy," a new voice said. She flinched. "Let me take him." Parker stepped through the back door. "He'll pay before he rots. You know he will."

She sniffed, nodded, and finally stepped back. "The blood was kind of making me queasy anyway."

Jesus. My woman. Laughter fell from my mouth. Charlie followed.

"Blackie?" I asked.

"Outside, cursing up a storm because he wanted a go at Switch and Poppy stole his weapon." So that was where she got the gun. Parker added, "He's fine. Lan's with him, and he'll call an ambo when we get Switch outta here."

"Of course my man is fine. Nothing can kill that bastard but me, and it'll come close for gettin' himself shot," Roda snapped from behind me.

"This won't be—" Switch started, until Charlie leaned over and knocked him out cold with one punch.

I met Parker's gaze. His brows lifted, and I nodded. "Compound first, then you can take him in."

"Use Blackie's van," Roda said as she stomped her way around and over things to get to the back door. "Just pull it up the drive to the back fence. Load him in that way."

Hell, had Roda had experience in loading up bodies?

That was something to think about another day. Charlie headed towards the front. "I'll get the van."

I made my way Poppy, stepping over the motherfucker on the floor, but also looking back to see if Mum was okay. She nodded, gesturing me on with a smile. In seconds, I had Poppy in my arms. I lifted her and walked us out the back door. Ignoring Roda chewing out Blackie, I put Poppy's feet down. She wrapped her arms around my neck and smiled up at me. "I didn't realise shooting someone was so freeing."

I jerked my head back in shock.

She laughed. "Doesn't mean I'll be doing it again." Her humour finished, she said, "I was so scared, Miah. Scared out of my mind I would lose all of you."

"I know, baby. I would have been too."

She snorted. "No. Hulk never gets scared."

Threading my hand into her hair, I tugged gently until I had her eyes. Touching my lips to hers, I then pulled back, and admitted, "When it comes to anything harming you, I'm scared."

"Then we'll protect each other."

"Yeah, we will."

By the time Switch was loaded, Vicious and Pick arrived to drive him back to the compound, and Roda was still letting Blackie have it when the ambo arrived.

The paramedics walked through the back fence, and since I was standing over Poppy while she sat with Blackie, who was sucking up the attention from her since his woman was a hard-arse, I felt Lan tense at my side. He'd been smirking down at the ground, amused by Roda and her ranting, but his gaze rose when we heard the gate. His body locked solid when he saw the ambos.

Two guys, one tall, the other shorter, and it was the shorter one who stumbled a step when he spotted Lan.

"East," Lan said.

The guy nodded, and quickly averted his eyes, then went about checking Blackie like his partner was. Something had happened between Lan and that East guy, and I wasn't the only one who noticed.

So did Parker. It caused his face to get serious as he watched Lan eyeing East. He shook it off and said, "Name's Parker. Jarrod Blackcomb was shot by an intruder in the shoulder."

"Looks like it's gone right through," East said. "Let's get you to the hospital to get stitched up."

"Didn't catch your name," Parker clipped.

"Easton Ravel."

"Didn't know you were back in town," Lan piped in.

Poppy caught my eyes and widened. She'd caught on that something was happening.

"Well, I am."

"East—"

"Sorry, can't talk. Oliver, let's get Mr Blackcomb up. Don't think we'll need the stretcher. Do we?" he asked Blackie.

"Fuck no, I can walk."

"Not for long," Roda mumbled.

"Can you give me a sedative?" Blackie questioned, moaning as he got to his feet with the help of the ambos.

"I'll get you set up with one in the ambulance," Oliver said.

Blackie snorted. "It ain't for me, boy. Think my

woman needs it so she'll stop givin' me shit for being goddamn shot."

Easton and Oliver gave each other a look, smiling. Lan's jaw clenched. Parker's eyes narrowed at Lan and the Easton guy.

I curled Poppy into me and kissed her forehead. What a goddamn day.

"See you soon," Parker called to me. I gave him a chin lift. Yeah, he'd see me soon, when he picked up Switch from the compound after I was done with him.

"You okay here with Mum?" I asked.

Her arms tightened around my waist. "Sure am."

She knew where I was going, what I was gonna do, and she didn't say anything about it.

Fuck me, but my woman was bloody heaven sent.

CHAPTER TWENTY-THREE

POPPY

"Jesus, woman," Jerimiah groaned, throwing his head back against the tiled wall. His hands threaded through my hair as I sucked down to the base of his cock. "Christ," he hissed. "Your mouth feels so damn good, baby." I wanted to grin, pleased with myself, but I didn't. I was busy. As water sprayed down from the shower over my back, I slowly dragged my mouth back up to the tip of his cock. I swirled my tongue around the end and looked up. My man was losing it. His jaw clenched so tightly it protruded the muscles on his neck. *Amazing.*

His head dipped down, meeting my gaze. His was

intense, darker than normal. One hand left my hair and came around to glide over my top lip as I took his cock down the back of my throat. "You like suckin' me." It wasn't a question; he knew I did. Still, I hummed anyway. His eyes flashed, and too soon he was dragging me up his body.

"I was enjoying that," I complained.

His lips twitched. "Know that, darlin'. Think you'd live with my cock in your mouth if you could." I nodded, my glare doing nothing to stop him. He turned us in the shower. My warm back hit the cool tiles and I gasped. His mouth slammed down on mine, and he picked me up, using his hands on my arse. I wound my legs around his hips.

"Look at me," he demanded. I brought my gaze from the ceiling down, my body finally used to the shock of the coldness against my back. He captured my gaze. "Gonna fuck my woman."

I nodded. "Please."

His hand back between us, I looked down and watched him take his cock in hand and hold it so the tip just touched my entrance.

"Watch us," he growled.

"I am."

"Watch," he clipped, and then thrust himself deep inside of me. I gripped his shoulders tightly and moaned. "Watch," he said again. I opened my eyes since they closed in the sensation of Jerimiah filling me wholly. He pulled out and slid back in slowly. "So wet," he groaned. "Fuck, Poppy. This is us."

"Yes," I cried when he pulled back out and thrust back in. "So good."

"Fuck yes."

"Miah," I whispered. He lifted his head and gave me what I wanted. His mouth on mine. His hands on my arse pressed in, holding me as he fucked me hard. I whimpered against his lips, and he growled in response. Breaking the kiss, I tilted my head back, only to bring it back and into the crook of his neck. There I licked, sucked and then bit.

"Hell, Poppy," Jerimiah grunted. His pace somehow picked up, driving into me fiercely.

"C-close," I said against his neck.

He braced me against the wall. I lost one hand off my butt, which he slid around to grip my breast. "Mouth," he ordered. I picked up my head after one last nibble, which caused him to shudder, and planted my lips against his. He opened for me. I teased my tongue with his. A pinch of my nipple took me over the edge. I wanted to pull back, to scream while my walls clenched around Jerimiah's cock still pumping in and out of me, but I didn't. Jerimiah liked to feel my moan, feel my breath panting, and take my whimpers into him.

"Fuck," he mumbled against my mouth. His body

tensed for all of a second. His hands gripped me tighter than before, and I caught his groaned release in my mouth, drinking it down as he shot his cum inside of me.

Slowing his thrust, he kissed me one last time and met my gaze. "Amazing each and every fuckin' time."

"It's because it's us."

He grinned. "Damn right."

AFTER THE SHOWER, we headed to the compound since Pick wanted to talk to Jerimiah about something. It'd been a couple of months since Switch showed and things were better than I could have imagined. I didn't ask what happened when Jerimiah went to the compound, and he didn't tell me. Though, I had overheard Switch ended up staying in the hospital for a long time due to his extensive number of injuries until he was fit enough to go to jail.

Jerimiah took my hand, helping me off his ride before he climbed off himself. We placed our helmets on the bike, knowing no one would mess with them or even come on to the compound property to thieve them... well, unless they wanted to be hunted and harmed.

Walking into the common room, I noticed it was busy. Brothers and most of the old ladies were mulling around either drinking, talking, playing pool, or eating.

Leanna was there, walking around with a food tray in her hand, offering it out to anyone who would take some.

"Is it some type of special day and we didn't get the memo?" I asked.

"Fuck," Jerimiah clipped low.

"Did you show her?" Dad asked, coming out of nowhere.

"Charlie, I said I wasn't doin' it until later."

"Show me what?" I asked.

Dad's eyes flashed, then he backed up a step. "Blame Roda and Leanna. It was their idea to throw this."

"Throw what?" I asked, honestly confused.

"What are you doin' here then?" Dad asked Jerimiah, ignoring me.

"Had to talk to Pick. Then I was gonna show her."

"Would someone tell me what I'm obviously supposed to see?" I demanded, throwing my hands to my hips.

Jerimiah sighed. He turned to face me, stepping right in front of me. He ran a hand through his hair, and chuckled. "Darlin', I was gonna surprise you with it this afternoon, but now I'll just have to tell you." He shot Dad an annoyed look.

"The women," Dad snapped, making it clear it wasn't his fault.

"What were you going to show me?"

"Our house. We're moving in together this weekend."

"Our house?" I whispered.

"Yeah, babe. A few weeks ago, we were on a ride and you said you'd like to live in that area since it was close to your dad. I found us a house there. One Charlie assured me you'd like."

"But... but..." My eyes flicked to my dad and then back to Jerimiah. "...Dad needs me at home."

Dad scoffed. I faced him, and Jerimiah slipped in behind me with his arms curling around me, one at my chest and waist. His usual embrace. Claiming.

"Honey, I'm your father, and the noises I hear sometimes are ones no father should hear." Dad flushed, but I was sure I was brighter than he was, while Jerimiah threw his head back and roared with laughter.

"They're moving in together. She ain't seen the house yet, but she agrees," Dad announced. Not that he really had my answer, but after hearing what he'd just said, I was keener to move out than I ever had been.

Cheers went up. Leanna came to us first and gave us both a hug since Jerimiah was still at my back. Roda and Blackie approached.

"Still not sure why we're celebrating this," Blackie grumbled. "They're practically living with each other already. It'll just be minus Charlie."

I felt Jerimiah chuckle at my back. "I'm not sure either Blackie. Not that I don't appreciate it," he quickly added when both Leanna and Roda glared at him.

Roda huffed. "Life's too short, gotta live it big, and

why not do it with a party? Celebrate the shit outta everything I say."

"Here, here," someone shouted.

It was later, while I was sitting on Jerimiah's lap on one of the couches talking to Manda who was on Muff's lap, when Pick, Billy, and Josie came up to Jerimiah. Manda and Muff had been inseparable. Any chance they got, they spent it together. I was happy to see not only one of Jerimiah's brother's so content, but my best friend too. She was so damn happy that she called me all the time about it.

"Gotta ask a favour, brother," Billy said. He pulled Josie close to his side with an arm around the neck. His fingers brushed against Pick on the other side of Josie. Pick grinned. He never did that much, but it did show more when he was around Billy or Josie.

Jerimiah stood, placing me on my feet, his hands going to my waist. "What's up?"

"We're heading out of town for a while. Goin' up to stay in Halls Gap at Dive's old place. Need someone to manage the bar."

Jerimiah stiffened. I glanced up at him. He was shocked by the offer. "Me?" he asked, and I grinned, matching Josie's smile.

"Yeah, brother." Billy chuckled.

"You've done a business degree at uni. Know you can handle things," Pick said.

"Shit. Well, yeah. I could do that." Shock was still evident in his light tone. "Thanks for trustin' me," he added.

"She's pregnant," Lissa, Dallas's woman and a friend of mine, yelled. "Shit. Shit, sorry. Sorry, I have a habit of telling people."

The brothers went wild over the news, while most of the women had tears in their eyes.

Pick and Billy chuckled, while Josie beamed in the middle of them. After the noise settled, Josie reassured Lissa, "Don't worry. We were going to say something tonight anyway."

"Does Nancy know?" I heard someone ask.

"Yes. She was the first person we told."

Pick snorted. "Surprised you didn't hear her screaming from here."

The brothers laughed. Nancy was Josie's adoptive mum. I had the chance to meet her when Josie and Nary took me to Ballarat. It was after things had cooled down with Switch, and also after Parker and Lan had caught the guy who'd been beating strippers. Apparently, it was a guy who was messed in the head, something about his mum being a stripper and him hating her for showing people her body. In turn, he hated all strippers.

Everyone had been both surprised and relieved that not only had the guy been caught, but that it wasn't a direct attack on the club. Jerimiah had told me they'd dedicated hours to finding the guy, and the whole time they'd focused on enemies of the club, completely missing the real threat. It was clear they'd been pissed by misdirecting their efforts, but still, it was over. And while I knew little about club business, I knew enough that the relief had been felt by all.

Someone's phone rang, others went about their business, but for some reason, I focused on whose phone it was.

Parker's.

"Yeah?" He stood. "What?" His body solidified. "I'm on my way."

"Brother?" Jerimiah called.

"A group of people entered Lan's home and beat the fuck outta him before his neighbour," his jaw clenched, "came to help him. Now he won't go to the goddamn hospital. I'm heading there to talk some sense into him."

Worry formed in my stomach.

"I'm coming," Jerimiah said.

"So am I," Muff said.

"You got us too," Billy said.

Parker gave them a chin lift and started for the door. Jerimiah turned me in his arms. "You okay?"

"Yeah, sure. Go. Help him talk with Lan. He seemed real pissed, Miah."

"He is. Not sure what's goin' on with those two. You all right to hold off seeing the house until later?"

"Of course. Your brother needs you."

His eyes warmed before I had his mouth against mine in a hard, searing kiss.

MUCH LATER, when Jerimiah came back to the compound without Parker, he interrupted my chat with Della, Handle's pregnant woman, with a kiss to my neck.

Smiling, I glanced up at him. "You okay?"

"Yeah, darlin'. Ready to see our house?"

"I sure am." I looked back to Della.

She grinned. "Go. We'll finish this another time."

"Thanks," I said, reaching over to give her hand a squeeze. She was sweet. Had been through hell, but she'd found her freedom in Handle, and they were going to have a baby together.

Walking to the ride, Jerimiah asked, "What were you two talking about?"

I shrugged. "Life, happiness, work."

"Work?" he said, while helping me with my helmet.

"Yeah, work. I'm tired of waiting tables, Jerimiah." The look of relief on his face had me laughing. "So," I drew out. "I asked Samuel if he needed a bookkeeper or an assistant, since I'd done an accounting course at uni. I hadn't mentioned it when I'd been interviewed because at the time, we needed the extra cash earned by the tips I made." His face screwed up. "Samuel's a nice guy, my Miah, one who knows *who* I belong to."

"Damn right," he clipped. "What did the dick say?"

"He's going to give me a try as his assistant. Means I'll be working behind the scenes."

"Thank fuck." Jerimiah grinned.

"Thought that would make you happy."

"Nah, darlin'. It's just you."

I gushed as my body filled with warm fuzzy feelings. My man was sweet. "And you know, even if I didn't like the house, I wouldn't care because I'd have you by my side. You're all that matters."

But of course, Jerimiah knew me well, and in the end, I did *love* the house. Which I showed him how much in nearly every room.

EPILOGUE

POPPY

A year later, I was at the bar with Mena on one side and Manda on the other, while they had their men crowding their backs and talking. My man was on the other side of the bar serving drinks. Pick and Billy decided to keep Jerimiah on as a manager while they set up another pub in a suburb on the other side of the compound. The businesses were thriving, which was good since Josie ended up pregnant with twins. She gave birth a few months ago to a boy named Theodore Richard Alexander, Theo for short, and a girl named Peyton Nancy Alexander. Both Pick and Billy changed their last names to match their woman's and children's.

No one was sure who the father actually was between the two of them, and honestly, it was hard to guess when you saw the babies. Not that it mattered to anyone, as long as they were happy, and they were.

Della and Handle were gifted with a baby girl too. Her name was Ashley Kaidion. Della and Handle married in a beautiful garden ceremony just before she was born.

Everyone around us was happy in life. I couldn't believe the amount of peace in, not only at the Hawks compound, but Venom's as well. Blackie and Dodge hadn't joined clubs, but it didn't mean we weren't all close still. If they needed Jerimiah's club at their back, they had it. No questions asked.

My eyes caught on the door opening. Lan, Parker, and Easton strolled in. Parker had his head thrown back in laughter. He was another person who used to always seem so straight-laced, even pissed at the world, but he'd been pissed for other reasons. Not only him, but Lan also. Well, until—

"Poppy," Manda called, clicking her fingers in front of my face, bringing me out of my thoughts.

"Yeah?"

"I said, Muff and I are getting a place not far from you."

I gasped. "Oh my God. Really?"

She laughed. "Yes. He's it for me."

Excited laughter bubbled up and out. "Aren't you glad you moved back?"

"Hell yes."

"Darlin'," Jerimiah called. I faced him.

"Did you hear the news?" I asked.

He chuckled. "Yeah, baby. Muff told me he was gonna ask your girl to move in with him."

I narrowed my gaze. "And you didn't think to tell me."

His brows rose. "Darlin'," was all he said. Still, I knew what he meant. It was bro-code. He grinned. "Got drinks to serve, but give me your hand."

My hand moved on its own, placing it in his over the bar. When I felt something slide on my finger, I looked down. My heart skipped a beat and tears filled my eyes. I glanced back up at my man. "Yes," I whispered.

He chuckled again. "Haven't even asked yet, my Poppy."

"Doesn't matter, my Miah. The answer will always and forever be yes."

His eyes heated. "First kiss here. Had to be here for this."

"I know." I nodded, my bottom lip trembling. I loved the thought of that, but it didn't matter where he proposed, because I'd be filled-to-the-brim blessed no matter.

"Love you, darlin'," he whispered.

Getting to my feet, I kneeled on the seat and reached

over, wrapping my arms around his neck. "Love you more and more each day, my Miah."

"She said yes," Manda squealed loudly.

MANY, MANY YEARS LATER.

FANG

"Dad," Nate called from down at my side. Our son. Loved our boy just as much as I did his ma. He was eight years old. It took us a few years of trying for Poppy to finally fall pregnant, and due to the sickness, pain, and nearly losing her, it had worried me so much I told her one was enough. Thankfully, she'd agreed. "Can I go and play outside with Hannah?" Hannah was Muff and Manda's girl, a year younger than Nate.

"Are there any brothers out there?"

He rolled his eyes. "Yes."

"All right, but keep an eye on Hannah."

He straightened, taking on the responsibility. "I will."

He took off running, meeting a smiling Hannah at the back door. I saw Koda, Dive and Mena's boy standing there too. He gave me a chin lift. Thirteen and already a biker in training.

We were in the compound to celebrate Texas's birthday, as well as him being patched fully into the Hawks. He'd put things off for a few years to get his tattoo business set up.

Things had been goddamn amazing. Of course, there'd been a few hiccups along the way, some that put fear into us, but we all pulled through.

"Yo, Fang," Alvin called with a wave. He headed right for his sister and dad, hugging them both hello. It took some time, because Alvin had demons to work through about helping his mum, for everything to settle between the three of them. But he was finally back in the fold. Though, he never asked to be patched in to either Venom or Hawks again, which was good as Blackie or Dodge didn't want to take him in.

"She's not fuckin' doin' it," Talon snarled as he passed my way in a stride. His woman quickly followed with a scowl on her face.

"She's responsible and old enough to do this, Talon Marcus."

He stopped, turned and got in Zara's face. "I nearly lost my girl. *Lost her*. I will not have her fuckin' leavin' to go overseas."

Shit. It was obvious he was talking about Maya, and I couldn't blame him for not wanting her outta his sight after what happened.

Zara sighed and wrapped her arms around his neck. "I

know, honey. I do. It's scary, but teaching her to fear the what-ifs isn't the way to go."

"Christ," he bit out. Then he sighed, running a hand over his face. "If Swan's going for sure, I'll think about it again."

Zara smiled, kissed her man, and then ran off to where some of the women were gossiping.

An arm wrapped around my waist. I lifted mine and Poppy snuggled in close.

"You happy?" she asked.

"Can never not be happy with you and Nate in my life."

"Good answer, Hulk."

I curled her in further, so her front was flush with my own. "Love you, my Poppy."

"Love you, my Miah."

Leaning in, I took her mouth, and...

"Gross. Mum, Dad, stop kissing," Nate called. We glanced over to our son, who was already caked in mud. "I'm never doing that with a girl *or* a boy like Uncle Beast and Knife and Uncle Parker—"

"Nate," Charlie called. "Don't you worry about that stuff yet, son. And no matter which way you go, we'll all love you."

And that was the damn truth right there.

Out Gamed (novella) (Nancy and Gamer's story)

Outplayed (novella) (Violet and Travis's story)

Romantic comedies

Making Changes

Making Sense

Fumbled Love

Trinity Love Series

Left to Chance

Love of Liberty (novella)

Paranormal

Death (with Justine Littleton)

In The Dark

CONNECT WITH LILA ROSE

Webpage: www.lilarosebooks.com

Facebook: http://bit.ly/2du0taO

Instagram: www.instagram.com/lilarose78/

Goodreads:

www.goodreads.com/author/show/7236200.Lila_Rose